MW01488566

Banned From Public Radio

Michael Graham

Pinpoint Press
Columbia, South Carolina

Banned From Public Radio.
Copyright © 1995 by Michael Graham.
Published by Pinpoint Press,
A Belesprit Enterprise.

All rights reserved. Printed in the United States of America. No part
of this book may be reproduced in any manner whatsoever without
written permission except in the case of brief quotations embodied in
critical articles or reviews. For information, address Pinpoint Press,
Post Office Box 5146, Columbia, South Carolina 29250; or via e-mail
at Navigator9@aol.com.

ISBN 0-9648553-0-5

Library in Congress Cataloging-In-Publication Data available.

ACKNOWLEDGMENTS

The author would like to thank the following people for their help and support:

John Wrisley, for getting this project off the ground; my wife Jennifer, for not shooting it down; Amy Whitaker Singmaster, publisher and practicing Libertarian of the *Free Times*, for excusing a hundred missed deadlines; Secretary of State Jim Miles, who refused to fire me despite almost daily requests; Ben Rast, for help above and beyond the call of duty; Powell, Stan, Dana, Janna, Lani, Michael, Christian, Wesley, Scott and KPC for edits, suggestions and criticisms of the contents herein; Bob Pierce, Debra-Lynn Hook, Ann Humphries, Dean Dubois, Judy Thomason, Wanda Jewell and all the successful writers and book sellers who helped me produce this volume, proving yet again the truth of Graham's Rule #1: No idea is too good to steal.

This book is humbly dedicated to Hugh, Verne, Ernie, Kay and the rest of the 1995 South Carolina General Assembly. Without their extreme efforts, this book would not have been possible.

Or necessary.

Table of Contents

Carolina On My Mind   1
Banned From Public Radio • Sweet Carolina Girls
It's Hard To Be A Saint In The City • High Rollers
Southern Hospitality • Judge Not • Can't Touch This
Here She Is... • Bowled Over

Clinton and Me   27
Clinton And Me • Don't Jump! • BureauBubba
Every American's Right • Let Us Pray
Clinton and Me, Two

Guys And Dolls   43
Get Me To The Church On Time • A Woman's Place
Knock On Woody
I Can't Give You Anything But Love
Bad Boys • Time Off For Good Behavior
Have Yourself a Gender-Neutral Christmas

Radio Ga Ga   61

Television That Preaches and Conspires • Shut Up
Culture Bores • The Butthead Made Me Do It
Motivational Speaking • Radio Ga Ga
It's a Wonderful Lie

P.C.   81

Church Chat • Hooters • Veg Out
High School Confidential • Boomers
Workin' For a Livin' • Finished
Thank God for Hitler

In The News   101

O'Justice • God's Geeks • Blowed Up Real Good
Washington Huskies • School's Out
The Last Bus To Hell • Real Losers

Who, Me?   117

In The Family Way • Stop, Thief! • The Name Game
Check, Please • Book Learnin' • A Bit of Humbug

Chapter 1

CAROLINA ON MY MIND

BANNED FROM PUBLIC RADIO

Banned.

The first time I can remember being banned was in the fifth grade. Mrs. Storey, my teacher at Pelion Elementary School, had given us a writing assignment, the nature of which I cannot recall. I do recall, however, Mrs. Storey's angry reaction to my composition, though my classmates considered it a "yuk-filled laugh-fest" (as reviewed by my friend Bill Wetzel), "guaranteed to make Joyce Stover wet her pants!"

As I recall, the essay dwelled heavily on the topic of pants-wetting and other bodily functions, functions which the reactionary Mrs. Storey felt did not meet community standards. "You have gone too far this time, Michael," she scolded me. "Do not read one more word of that filth in my class."

Since then, I have rarely escaped the censor's wrath. A senior-class photo I organized was confiscated by my high school principal.

BANNED FROM PUBLIC RADIO

As a student at Oral Roberts University, I was barred from writing for the school newspaper. Cartoons and literary contraband that I posted on my dorm room door were regularly confiscated by school administrators.

When I was chosen by the English Department of Oral Roberts to edit the fine arts magazine, the university censored the entire issue and refused to allow it to go to press. Later, when I ran for student body president, the dean of students announced that I was on some form of double-secret "attitudinal probation," a level of discipline so covert that I had apparently spent several years being punished without knowing it. Interestingly, there was only one prohibition placed on people serving this mysterious "attitudinal probation": you were not allowed to run for student body president.

Even in the avant-garde world of stand-up comedy, where I made my living for six years, I could not avoid attempts at censorship. I was opening for Jerry Seinfeld at Zanie's, a comedy club in Nashville, making fun of the "rouge-naped" rubes who make up the citizenry of Tennessee, when a local gentleman leapt to his feet and shouted, "He's makin' fun of our heritage! Y'all gonna let him make fun of our heritage?"

I did what any stand-up comic worth his two-drink minimum would do: I laid into them even more. While most of the crowd enjoyed it, the local and his seven (count 'em, SEVEN) friends got more and more angry...a condition that worsened when people at neighboring tables began explaining my jokes to them.

When my show ended, the party of eight gathered at the stage exit and were prepared to give me a good ol' fashioned Rocky Top welcome. I had to be escorted to the dressing room to avoid bloodshed.

Given my history, why was I surprised when, after three appearances on South Carolina Educational Radio Network's *Dateline: Carolina* program, I was banned from public radio?

Honestly speaking, I find it disconcerting to be "banned" from anything. Censored, perhaps, or invited not to return, sure. But banned? Being banned means not only do you find my recent work offensive, but that I have shown such a complete lack of decency that

2

you cannot imagine a future moment when I might behave appropriately.

Forget "Don't call us, we'll call you." Banned is "I don't think you should be allowed to have a phone."

And to be banned from *public* radio?

PBS is hardly a crusader of community standards and viewer sensibilities. Public radio and television regularly broadcast material that would make a junior high gym teacher blush. Graphic sexual discussion, unashamed defenses of Communist totalitarianism, Mark Russell's piano playing--no matter how offensive, there is nothing public radio won't broadcast.

Except me.

What did I say to cause so much trouble? The following is my commentary as it aired on September 24, 1991 on the South Carolina Educational Radio Network:

You can come out now, they're gone.

Yes, the South Carolina General Assembly has once again retreated into the woods, their top-secret, one-day, "quick-before-anyone-figures-out-what-we're-doing" mission accomplished. While most of the day was spent with mundane chores such as sustaining vetoes and erasing Ron Cobb's number from the Rolodex, the primary reason for this special matinee performance was the 1991 Ethics Act, now destined by God and Carroll Campbell to become law.

As you all know, the ethics bill was the single most important piece of legislation of the year, the number one priority of both parties...so naturally everyone went home without voting on it. And with good reason.

Unlike most of the meaningless edicts passed by the Assembly, either declaring April "Turnip Month" or making Beef-A-Roni the state pasta, an ethics law could actually affect the way our state is run. So the great minds at Main and Senate decided they needed a few weeks to think it over...give them time to test drive the loopholes and see how they fit.

Unable to find a way out, the courageous women and men of the General Assembly enacted a tough, new Ethics Act. It is now a crime in the state of South Carolina to get caught.

But why? Why convene an expensive and unnecessary special session to pass a single bill? I know the legislators agreed to give up their per diems and survive an entire day in Columbia on nothing more than complimentary happy hour hot wings, but why convene at all? Why not just wait until next year and, between pig pickin's and okra struts, find a minute to vote on this nonsense and let it go?

After all, nobody in South Carolina cares about ethics, least of all the voters. We've proven over the years that we will elect just about anybody this side of Al Capone. We're the people who re-elected John Jenrette. Remember John "The Cash Is In The Shoebox" Jenrette, who was called upon to serve by the people of Horry County despite the fact that he was already "serving" in the Federal Department of Rock Breaking and License Plate Art?

Then there's the legend of Gene Carmichael:

For those of you unfamiliar with Palmetto State folklore, legend has it that Gene Carmichael was a mythical state senator from Dillon who went to jail for buying votes. Then, after serving his sentence, he was promptly re-elected running on his "Next Time I'll Share the Loot!" platform. According to legend, Senator Carmichael roams the halls of the State Senate today and was recently seen voting on a bill to bring ethical government to South Carolina.

This, of course, is just a story. None of it could be true. Spending a year debating an ethics package and allowing a convicted felon to hold state office and vote on it, why, that would be as ridiculous as, say, allowing lawyer/legislators to practice law before the same agencies these legislators regulate!

This rush to bring ethics to state government is misguided. If we prevent criminals from serving in state government, we won't have enough people left to convene a quorum. And who would provide the kind of entertaining election campaigns South Carolinians have come to expect?

Ethics in government-Hah! What's next? Morality in religion?

4

That's it. No call to arms, no threats or slander, nothing that couldn't be repeated at a tent meeting, Baptist revival or even a Rotary club. Only my comment that maybe, just *maybe*, passing an ethics bill that had the whole-hearted endorsement of a felon convicted for ethics violations was not worth getting into a sweat about. That was my opinion, anyway.

It was not, however, the opinion of the General Assembly, that happy, fun-loving crowd of gregarious public servants who always enjoy a good joke, even at their own expense. A couple of those nutty legislators got on the phone to the state-employed bureaucrats at SCERN and said: "That Graham guy is a hoot! We've got a little joke of our own and it goes like this: these two ETV employees walk into a Senate budget conference...and are never heard from again! You got it?"

I was banned the next day.

That's when I learned that it's not "public radio" at all, but rather "state-run radio." You know, like *Pravda*...

Alas, the story does not end here:

After being banned from radio, I began writing occasional articles for magazines and humor columns for various weeklies in the Southeast. Then in 1993, I was hired by the South Carolina Secretary of State's office as its communications director. It seemed a perfect match: I enjoy writing and I enjoy politics, and for two years I worked for the state and wrote my columns and was generally happy as a clam. I was even asked to do commentary on the 1994 elections for a commercial AM station. I thought I had it made.

Oh, how soon we forget...

I forgot, for example, what the lackeys at state-run radio tried to teach me, which is "never cheese off the people who write the checks." Politicians who didn't like my commentaries began making comments of their own. One legislator, upon finishing one of my columns, was quoted as saying "Who the hell does Michael Graham think he is?" Another warned that I "wasn't doing myself any favors" in the General Assembly.

And so, believe it or not, the entire legislative branch of the state government of South Carolina used up taxpayers time to pass a law firing me--specifically--from state government. It took an entire series of budget amendments, but they did it:

They banned me from South Carolina.

I ought to be upset (my landlord certainly isn't happy about it), but I just can't stop laughing. The idea that a group of adults would go to all this trouble over a few smart remarks...well, let's just say that if pettiness were a capital crime, there are legislators desperately awaiting a last-second phone call from the Governor.

Meanwhile, I've written the book, which you're now holding, a collection of the outrageous, offensive and dangerous columns that have gotten me into so much trouble. Enjoy them.

And remember: If you can't laugh at yourself, you are well on your way to a successful career in American politics.

August, 1995

SWEET CAROLINA GIRLS

"I never had any doubt that this young girl was intelligent, but being intelligent can indicate a little deviousness."--11th Circuit Solicitor Donnie Myers, referring to confessed murderer and would-be Harvard alum, Gina Grant.

There are a million stories on the mean streets of South Carolina, and they are all about women.

Strong women. Hard women. Tough-talkin', rough-ridin', butt-kickin', Momma-beatin', lake-drivin', Citadel-goin' women who know what they want and who to kill to get it.

It was synchronicity that brought matricidal Gina Grant and would-be coed Shannon Faulkner to the front pages in the same week, the former for getting booted from Harvard, the latter for being admitted to The Citadel. They are both tough, determined and bright...though I have to disagree with Solicitor Myers' assessment of Ms. Grant.

"Intelligent" people do not murder their moms by hitting them in the face thirteen times with a lead candleholder and then try to make it look like a suicide! ("Farewell, cruel world [wham!] Life isn't worth living [wham!] I'm going to end it all [wham!] I'm starting to feel woozy..." [wham!])

Intelligence is in short supply for Ms. Faulkner as well, who told a reporter that one reason she had wanted to go to The Citadel was the fabled alumni network. "I realize now that network is never going to work for me," she moaned.

Well, what did she think was going to happen? Did she plan on being named "Citadel Grad Most Likely To Become Pregnant" and live happily ever after at Beauregard, Hampton and Maybank, Attorneys-at-Law?

In the same interview, she said that her late adolescence has been "ripped from me" because of her decision to go The Citadel, and she bemoaned missing the normal college experience. Once again, this is what you might expect to happen when you attend an institution you are actively attempting to destroy.

Nothing against Ms. Faulkner. I think she should be able to go there, though I can't imagine why she would want to. Citadel whiners who talk about how a woman will lower The Citadel's "high standards" have little credibility given that current Citadel admissions requirements are:

A: "Who's your Daddy?" and
B: "Where's his checkbook?"

Cita-dullards earnest about maintaining high standards and a single-sex status could solve all their problems by having strenuous physical and academic requirements for admission. But that will never happen because those requirements would not only keep out women, but would also lock out the lard-butted larvae of wealthy alums.

Gina Grant, on the other hand, is going to have an admissions problem wherever she goes, given the quirky attitude parents and administrators tend to have about murderers attending their kid's day classes. Grant's defenders argue that her life should not be ruined just because of a "youthful indiscretion." (In my day, a "youthful indiscretion" was when my girlfriend's dad walked in while the two of us were on the pool table.)

Grant's advocates protest that ruining Gina's life would be unfairly adding tragedy to tragedy. But no one is advocating "ruining her life." Not being able to go to Harvard is not the same as being forcibly sentenced to barber college. Grant will still get a college education, she just won't get the elite college experience she might have had if she hadn't hideously murdered a family member.

Seems reasonable to me.

In fact, I know how we can kill two birds with one stone: Send Faulkner to Harvard and Grant to The Citadel! Shannon wants to teach English, right? Well, the Citadel is hardly the apex of the literary arts, the English Department in the School of Foreign Languages. Why not send her to Harvard, where she'll get a hero's welcome from the Yankee leftists and a real diploma to boot?

Meanwhile, Gina Grant could get her college education and simultaneously become a productive citizen as the first female Citadel cadet. What reason could possibly be raised to keep her out of the long, gray line? She's too demure? Not tough enough?

I'd like to see some cadet try that "weaker sex" stuff on Ms. Grant: "What? You don't think I can handle it, jarhead? Well, when was the last time *you* beat someone to death with a decorative household accessory, huh buddy?"

Carolina girls, the best in the world.

April, 1995

IT'S HARD TO BE A SAINT
IN THE CITY

Puritanism--the nagging fear that someone, somewhere, is having a good time.--H.L. Mencken

OK, OK, let's see if I've got this straight: We've got a successful and wildly popular St. Patty's Day festival. It receives no tax money whatsoever, but brings thousands of people into the city's prime retail district where they pump $5 million dollars into the local economy while supporting local artists, listening to local musicians and generally having a grand time. Therefore, we have to shut it down.

Yep, we're in Columbia all right.

Columbia: "The Mayberry of the Midlands," "The Cultural Vacuum on the Congaree," where night life is an oxymoron, where Continental Cuisine means a bag of pork rinds in the back of a '79 Lincoln. In a city like this, it's amazing City Council didn't try to kill the festival long ago.

Looked at from the viewpoint of a "traditional" Columbian (i.e., some old fart in Shandon whose house is paid for and who hasn't gone out after dark since the Ford Administration), the Five Points festival goes against every accepted norm of local life.

First of all, the St. Patty's Day festival receives no public funds. That means no petty special interest can bully the organizers by threatening to take away city money. Such events are threatening in a political hotbed like Richland County, where there are some 4,295 incorporated townships within the county limits. These duchies are largely populated by paranoid people willing to pay the higher taxes of a non-consolidated government just so they can reserve the right to keep "coloreds" from moving into the neighborhood.

A festival that is exempt from city government "sucking-up" ordinances is particularly unnerving to the current city leadership, whose motto is: "What's the point of having a public event if we can't jerk anyone around?" If you recall, these are the great brains who chased away the NFL for fear that local residents might foolishly

9

spend their Sunday afternoons watching professional football, rather than enjoying the new $300 million "MayorBob Memorial Ice Rink/Convention Center/Monorail/Jungle Safari Theme Park" soon to be built downtown.

The second problem with St. Patty's Day is that it is essentially a pro-business event. It promotes shopping, spending and even (occasionally) suds-slurping, all at retail establishments catering to the free-market desires of thousands of happy visitors. Yes, a few merchants shut down on St. Patty's Day, but the pennies lost in immediate sales are insignificant compared to their market exposure. But most Five Points merchants thrive on the Festival's success, which is why they choose to continue funding each year.

Tragically, Columbia's city leaders are not interested in business success. Having finally turned downtown Main Street into a vacant movie lot from "Schindler's List," the MayorBob Brain Trust is targeting Five Points, home of the festival. If the mayor's magic strikes again, Five Points could become the largest retail wig shop in North America.

But the third, and most serious, problem facing the St. Patty's Day festival is geography. Devine Street. Saluda Street. Shandon. These are upscale, influential neighborhoods. If the noisy crowds and double parkers were congregating on streets with names such as Confederate, Elmwood or North Main, city council would spend their next meeting finding ways to put parking meters in downtown toilet stalls instead of shutting down St. Patrick's Day. But because drunks occasionally urinate on the azaleas of the affluent, action must be taken at once.

For the true Columbian, revelry has no place. It makes them nervous. It bothers the cat. It disrupts their favorite episodes of Matlock. "If I wanted to live in a real city," they grouse, "I'd move!"

Thus, the St. Patty's Day festival, as it is today, cannot survive. It runs counter to the efforts of our city's prominent citizens who are committed to turning Columbia into a city entirely populated by elderly, middle class white people who pay no property taxes and spend their evenings staring out the window at the Confederate flag.

Why have St. Patrick's Day when you can have Utopia?

April, 1994

HIGH ROLLERS

The state budget is busted. President Clinton is about to send federal tax rates higher than Sam Donaldson's hair line. South Carolina is cutting back so much, members of the General Assembly may have to start buying their own drinks.

Desperate times call for desperate measures.

It's time for...THE LOTTERY!

Yes, that's right. I, Mr. Reactionary Conservative, Mr. Politically Incorrect, Mr. Gladiator and Slave Girl..(Well, uh, that's another story), am calling for South Carolina to join our neighbors in Georgia and vote ourselves a state-run lottery.

Why?

It's not because our state government is desperate for cash to help fund programs such as "Rural Legislator's Illiteracy Fund," and "Research for Advanced Gubernatorial Hair Maintenance"— although it is.

It's not because we are about to dump millions across the border into Georgia's treasury now that they have voted themselves the "Babylon of the Bible Belt"— although we are.

And it's not because South Carolinians already gamble millions each year on everything from cock fighting to buying mobile homes during tornado season— though, of course, we do.

I support a lottery because it is morally right and fiscally brilliant. A lottery is simply the ideal form of taxation: a voluntary tax on the stupid.

In a single stroke, the lottery does everything a good tax policy should do. It takes money from people who don't deserve to keep it, i.e., people stupid enough to buy lottery tickets, and relieves the tax burden on more intelligent (and presumably more productive) citizens. Even better, the lottery is completely free of the coercive elements of traditional taxation: No one is FORCED to pay!

This last element, the inability to audit, examine and/or terrorize citizens, is why people in the state tax offices oppose the lottery ("You mean, if they *don't* buy any lottery tickets, we still can't foreclose on their property? Then what's the point?"). The lottery, as a voluntary tax, points out the dirty secrets of our current tax system:

Taxes are currently collected by force of arms. Pay up or face the firing squad...or jail, anyway. Rather than being collected at the point of a gun, however, lottery "taxes" are collected at the end of a bottle, usually a beer bottle, at about 1:00 a.m. when you're stumbling into a convenience store looking for a microwave burrito.

Taxes are currently dumped into the "general fund," most of which is immediately converted into "general fraud" to pay off a friendly "general contractor," all of which is generally kept secret from the "general public." Lottery proceeds, on the other hand, are targeted for specific spending, usually education. This policy assures the voluntary taxpayer that, instead of paying off some worthless highway department lackey, part of every lottery dollar will go to pay off some worthless *education department* lackey.

Given the current ethical climate in government, this is a major step forward.

I have heard a variety of arguments against the lottery, all of them specious and indefensible. Some argue that we shouldn't have a government-run Lottery Department because it would tend to corrupt state officials. This implies that "corrupt state officials" are to be avoided and is, therefore, a direct challenge to our entire political system.

Others oppose legalized gambling with the usual do-gooders sense of self-righteousness: "Yes, stupid people do play the lottery," they argue," which is precisely why we must stop it. It is our duty to protect the intellectually-challenged from themselves."

This is the most unfair, unconscionable, un-American position taken since the Founding Fathers voted down the turkey as our National Bird. What right do we have to deny stupid people from expressing their hard-earned ignorance? The right to be dumb is the force behind the human longing for democracy, it is the one true human desire that binds us as a nation.

Why did the Eastern Europeans break through the Berlin Wall? Why have millions fought and died for democracy? For the right to think great thoughts, to create great art, to live challenging, risk-filled lives?

Of course not! People covet democracy because it allows them to be as stupid as they choose without direct government intervention, without the fear of having someone smack them upside the head for being so incredibly dumb.

The standard of freedom for many Americans is the right to be as stupid as possible and still live; to hug that fine line where, if they knew one fact fewer, were a single IQ point less attentive, they would be incapable of sustaining life. This is the ultimate aim of the self-governed. The mantra of the masses isn't "Protect me from my ignorance"; it's "Beer, Sex and Lotto...and Keep 'Em Coming!"

Ban the lottery because it takes advantage of stupid people? Then why not ban boxing? Used-car salesmen? The Democratic Party?

I am 100 percent American. Give me lottery, or give me death.

May, 1993

SOUTHERN HOSPITALITY

Growing up in rural South Carolina taught me the great lessons of Southern life:

Never trust a Yankee. Put salt, not sugar, on your grits. Respect your elders. Obey your parents. Date your cous..let's skip that one.

I also learned the classic tradition of Southern manners. Wipe your feet before you come in the trailer. Never take the last pork chop from the plate. Don't unbutton the top of your pants at the dinner table until AFTER your host has done so.

And, whatever you do, do not offend a guest. This gentility is the heart of the legendary "Southern Hospitality."

It is from this context that I approach the brouhaha surrounding the flying of the Confederate Battle Flag atop the South Carolina state house, and its appearance on the Georgia state flag.

The argument over the "Stars and Bars" has gone on ad nauseam with no discernible change in anyone's opinions. After years of wrangling, name-calling and deal-making, we still have the same intractable groups: a small minority who consider the flag an emblem of hate and racism; an even smaller minority who love the old Confederacy so much they are prepared to march North and re-take Richmond; and the rest of us, that large majority for whom the question: "Should the Flag Fly?" is slightly less important than the question: "Cornbread or rolls?"

We are tired and annoyed by this ongoing argument. One reason we are annoyed is that, on both sides, the discussion is dominated by kooks. Take a look at the audience in the typical "Pro-Flag" rally, and you'll find belt buckles outnumbering teeth three-to-one. The "Heritage--Not Hate" bumper sticker adorning South Carolina 4X4's is frequently accompanied by other insightful bon mots such as "I Don't Give A Damn How They Do It Up North," and "They Can Take My Chew When They Pry It Out of My Cold, Dead, Cancer-Riddled Jaws." These Southern loyalists are quick to note that the "Stars and Bars" was never meant to represent the Klan, but it's hard to take them seriously when they have the "Burning Cross Hibachi Set" in the back of the pick-up.

The other side has kooks, too. How else do you explain the ludicrous proposal to fly the African Nationalist Flag on the South Carolina state house? The second-rate Farrakhans pushing this idea make the Bubba crowd look like Brainiacs. Fighting the "racism and division" of the Confederate flag by flying the notoriously pro-Communist ANC's logo is like fighting lung disease by passing out free cigarettes.

The primary argument raised against the flag is, of course, racism. To extreme elements in the black community, the Battle Flag is just a swastika with a face lift. These people unthinkingly reduce the entire Civil War legacy to the question of slavery, and this clearly irrational position weakens their otherwise valid claims. Even their most sympathetic supporters in the white community know the war was about more than just slavery.

It is simply not the case that every person who supports the Confederate flag is a Klu-Kluxer, a truck driver or a sheep chaser. (An aside: I cannot count the number of times I've met some redneck Goober at the local fillin' station who doesn't know who his congressman is, or understand even the most primitive mathematics. But raise the issue of the flag, and ol' Goob will list the entire Confederate Cabinet under Jeff Davis, recount the daily movements of the Army of the Potomac from 1861-1864 and tell you the precise number of infantrymen who caught the clap serving in Hooker's Army).

For many South Carolinians, the Confederacy, more particularly the ante-bellum South, represents a golden age of civilized society. Yes, the unforgivable blight of slavery stains the memory, but in many ways the culture of the Old South--grace, manners, honor, courage--is worth celebrating. For thousands of its supporters, that is what the flag represents, and for these people the charges of racism and bigotry will not fly.

It is this "golden age" and its ethos, however, that present the flag supporters with an unanswerable dilemma: As a young Southern lad, I learned that it was an unpardonable sin to insult a guest. That simply isn't done down South. Up North, those Yankees talk loud, cuss in your face and make fun of your Momma, but not down here. We know better. We *are* better. This is part of the culture we celebrate with the flag.

However, the flying of the flag is, in itself, an insult to South Carolina's black citizens, neighbors and guests. Yes, their arguments against the flag are often self-serving. Yes, they would lose a referendum on the issue in a rout. But that is irrelevant. The fact remains that some our visitors, our neighbors and friends will certainly be offended.

It is our duty, therefore, as celebrants of the Southern culture, to remove the flag.

I think of my grandparents in rural Horry county who grew up with the "N" word as part of their vocabulary. They used it their entire lives without a hint of malice. However, as they grew older, they sensed that their black neighbors were offended by this word, no matter the intent of the user, and my grandparents simply dropped it. They did this, not because they felt they had done something wrong, not as an admission of racism, but because as Southerners, they were unwilling to needlessly cause offense.

True Southern hospitality.

March, 1995

Judge Not

Every thinking adult eventually comes to the realization that we live in a world without justice.

"The rain," the Good Book noted long ago, "falleth on the just and the unjust," and things haven't improved much since. In biblical times, the Lord Himself occasionally leveled the playing field by covering some self-satisfied, pompous jerk with boils, or turning him into a condiment. Today, the continuing boil-free prosperity of Geraldo Rivera and Leeza Gibbons calls into question the very existence of a just God.

Societies like ours try to circumvent the Lord's judicial inattentiveness by dishing out something called "social justice," but there is no such thing. Social justice is merely society's ability to pick its victims. And if you find yourself before the wrong South Carolina judge, you could be victim number one.

In our state, judges are elected by members of the General Assembly, who tend to choose fellow lawmakers. Therefore, to be a judge in South Carolina, you only have to be as intelligent as the most stupid legislator. Why not be as honest as the most ethical used-car salesman, or as virginal as the most chaste sorority sister?

The results of our politically-driven justice system can be seen behind the benches of South Carolina courts, and they ain't pretty. Former Representative and current redneck Hicks (yes, that's really his name) Harwell was elected judge after receiving a failing grade from the state Bar association and a panel of fellow lawmakers. The panel noted that Harwell's answers to simple legal questions "were on average rambling and had little relationship to the precise question that was asked," and "often included legal terms and concepts that did not relate to the questions."

Yep, he's a politician all right.

Another former legislator and current court embarrassment is The Honorable Danny Martin (D., Moronville) who was re-elected to the bench after receiving the lowest score ever on the judicial review exam. Though it is unusual for a judge to have his decisions reversed by higher courts, Martin has been overturned more often than a squad car during the LA riots. Even the 1994 Bar Survey of practicing attorneys found Martin deficient in "legal skills, impartiality, judicial temperament, industriousness and promptness."

Other than that...

Judge Martin does have his defenders, though they readily admit he knows little about the law. "I know that understanding the law is important," confessed a Martin admirer, "but understanding the people that come before him is important." The theory here is that Martin's race and socio-economic status (he's black and from a modest background) are more important than his knowledge of obscure legal jargon such as "witness" and "objection."

So we allow an incompetent to mete out justice to make up for society's past injustices.

At least Judge Martin can read and write. The same cannot necessarily be said for Judge Ernest White, a high school drop-out who at the time of this writing is inflicting the law from behind the bench of a South Carolina magistrate's court. When state law changed to require all magistrates have at least the equivalent of a high school diploma, Judge White lied about graduating from high school, then signed up to take the GED exam.

Now, the "standards" of the GED are such that a passing grade means your sentences occasionally contain a verb and your knowledge of history is comprehensive back to the beginning of the current baseball season. However low these standards may be, they were not low enough for Judge White.

It seems the good judge may have cheated on his GED. On the day of his exam, a state employee with a college degree happened to take the test as well. Why someone with a B.A. would spend a Saturday taking the GED is unclear ("Hey, Honey! They're giving standardized tests down at the V.F.W...Grab your #2 pencil and let's party down!"). Even more amazing, the drop-out Ernest White passed the test, while Joe College took a dive.

Could it be that the Judge didn't do his own work? Add the unusual "coincidence" of a high-ranking official from the state Department of Education making an unprecedented appearance at the test site to personally pick up the exams, and the fact that Judge White is married to a legislator and, well, where's Oliver Stone when you need him?

So South Carolina is left with one judge who's picking up pointers from episodes of *Matlock*, another who thinks "ad hominem" is part of a recipe for grits, and an illiterate. For the next several years, they will be deciding some of the most important issues in the everyday lives of the citizens who come before them seeking justice, people like you and me. Because the legislators of our state lack the will to reform the judicial selection process, these three stooges will decide who to imprison and who to set free; who will prosper and who will pay; who will be a parent and who will live alone. And they will issue these verdicts with the judicial expertise and sagacity one would expect to find in your average bus boy or fertilizer salesman.

In South Carolina, that's what we call "justice."

February, 1995

CAN'T TOUCH THIS!

While wandering through the state house in Columbia recently, I accidentally stumbled into a press conference being held by the South Carolina PTA. One of the hefty hausfraus hosting this shindig mistook me for a reporter (the press was conspicuous by its absence) and shoved a press release into my hands.

Never in a hurry to get back to the office, I lingered to hear the PTA's pitch. They were violently opposed to the "draconian cuts" in education being considered by the General Assembly, which was hardly a surprise from this PTA gathering where "T's" were outnumbered by "P's" by a wide margin. "We ain't got no money now," wailed one attendee, no doubt a public school grammarian on her lunch break.

As they talked, I looked over the list of proposed cuts that threatened to return our children to barbarism: $1 million dollar cut in new library books and $2 million out of "initiatives to involve families and parents in the schooling of their children." Initiatives, perhaps, like coming down to the Capitol and begging for more school money.

Now, you may be thinking that $2 million dollars is a lot of money to cut, but there is another, more important number to keep in mind: $1.97 BILLION dollars. That's right: the drastic $2 million cut is actually 1/10th of 1 percent of South Carolina's state education budget. Add another $1.3 billion from the local level and you'll see that what the General Assembly is proposing is hardly a cut at all; more like a scrape.

Yet these cuts were attacked as though school children were about to be flung into the streets, or worse, a church. These cuts are attacked because the attackers oppose any cuts in any government spending for any reason. And it's not just education: cuts in social programs, the arts, the General Assembly's polyester subsidy--every cow is sacred, every tax-funded trough must be defended to the death by well-fed bureaucrats.

The core question in the debate over tax relief is this: Is your state government a slim, trim Adonis who pinches every penny, or a bloated Bluto who blows our budgets on hooch and high living? And the obvious answer is the latter; that, as P.J. O'Rourke noted, "giving money and power to politicians is like giving beer and car keys to teen-aged boys."

It is an inarguable fact that our governments, state and local, have way too much money. The money they do have is spent badly, or lost to blatant fraud and abuse. Our PTA friends, for example, whine and cry about tiny cuts in pet projects. Meanwhile, South Carolina is spending an average of more than $5,000 per child in our public (read "government") schools. These schools suck up our money as fast as they can, take twelve years to crank out a class of semi-literate clods whose literacy level peaks with the question "Do you want fries with that?," then the school boards complain that they need more cash. Imagine the terrific education you could give your children for five grand apiece, and you'll see why government-run schools are a scam.

Not to pick on education. That's just one thing governments do badly. They aren't much better at delivering mail (post office), protecting children (DSS in Aiken County) or creating art (Strom Thurmond's post-modern hairdo).

What government *is* good at is creating more government. Since 1929, total government spending has grown seven times faster than the rate of inflation. Children born in 1900 spent approximately one-fifth of their lifetime earnings on government. Children born in 2000 will spend more than half. That means half of a lifetime spent funding a government that won't protect you on the street or educate your children, but will spend your money making sure country-club types can watch Masterpiece Theatre without paying for cable.

South Carolina's legislators have so much of your money to spend that, even after the proposed "draconian" cuts, this state will still have:

--11 state airplanes, more than any Southeastern state including Florida. And we only have *nine* constitutional officers. That means the entire state government could be airborne and we would still have two planes leftover to fly up liquor and party girls.

--$12 million dollars on the Division of Professional and Occupational Licensing, whose job is to throw any unauthorized haircutters, manicurists, tree growers or auctioneers into the hoosegow until they get a state permit.

--$200,000 on the Confederate Relic Room and Museum, where taxpayers offended by the battle flag can go to get really pissed off.

These examples go on and on, as do the demands that you fork over more of your money to the state. And you, the taxpayer, will never win because, while you are out earning your money, the teachers, bureaucrats and professional whiners who get it are at the state house lobbying for more.

One last statistic: How much of your tax money will state government spend next year?

All of it.

April, 1995

Here She Is...

I am here to defend the Miss South Carolina pageant.

To those philistines who incorrectly label this cultural event a "beauty pageant," I remind them it is a "scholarship pageant" as evidenced by the thousands of dollars awarded by South Carolina's most prestigious centers of learning. According to the pageant's press kit, our future Miss Mensa's compete for scholarships from institutions such as the University of South Carolina, Greenville Tech and the Sherman College of Straight Chiropractic.

Yes, the Miss South Carolina pageant is more than muscle tone. Consider the grueling "Interview" competition, when, armed with only an evening gown and a few bits of well-placed foam, our effervescent Einstein's tackle the toughest questions of the day with extemporaneous aplomb. Actually, "extemporaneous" may not be the right word. Each contestant is required to compose two essays, *either of which* might be chosen the night of the contest!

Obviously, advance preparation is impossible.

But beyond their minds, their insights and their bust lines, who are these women? To get the answers, I personally reviewed the resumes and essays submitted by each of the Miss South Carolina contestants. After several hours of reading, I came away with a new respect for the amount of humiliation people are willing to inflict upon themselves for a free ride to Chiropractic school.

Flipping through the resumes, I was struck by how well-traveled these women are. For example, Miss Lancaster is actually from Lexington, as is Miss Greenville. And Miss Hartsville. And Miss

Columbia. As for the actual Miss Lexington, none was listed, perhaps because no pageanteers were in town for the contest.

Along with Miss Charleston (from Columbia) and Miss South Congaree (Greer), there was Miss Coastal Empire of Gaston. Yes, the sleepy seaside fishing village of Gaston, where, as a little Miss, our contestant learned to sing from the fishermen who crooned as they cleaned the daily catch.

But these Bi-county beauties aren't just multi-addressed; they're multi-talented! The two-hour television show (yes, it seems longer to me, too) only highlights the more traditional talents such as singing, dancing and walking erect. However, according to their resumes (all are quoted verbatim and unadorned, I swear!), the competitive Miss of the 90's has mastered a wide range of difficult skills like:

Clogging (Miss Charleston), Shopping (Miss Marietta), raising Vietnamese Potbellied Pigs (Miss Gaffney), meeting people (Miss Southern 500--and without a net!), and skeet shooting (Miss Oconee), which I hope will eventually become part of the televised competition.

Most impressive: Miss Greenville, who "trained for the New York Marathon!" No indication that she actually *ran* in it, but who cares? She's already a winner!

Reading these personal resumes offered fascinating insights into the source of self-esteem for these dedicated competitors. Some touted glamorous genealogies ("I am a direct descendant of former United States president, John Tyler"--Miss Columbia North East) while others pointed to humble beginnings ("My house was built out of an old hog barn"--Miss Horry County).

Some had notable accomplishments ("I have been a licensed hair dresser since I was 18."--Miss Berkeley), and others, tales of terror ("I survived 10 days in Yosemite National Park...without cosmetics!"--Miss Wade Hampton-Taylors).

But these 40 points of light shine brightest in their submitted essays, powerful writings on the contemporary challenges facing our society:

"Education: A Possible Answer for AIDS?" queries Miss Easley from the cutting edge. And the haunting question from Hartsville: "Are We Breeding a Lost Generation?"

If we are, it certainly isn't because we haven't been warned. Miss Berea, an acute social observer, notes in her essay: "Families, in the United States, are becoming increasingly common."

While most of the essays centered on general statements ("Alcohol is a Dysfunctional Family"--Miss North Myrtle Beach, and "Life or Death: A Critical Choice"--Miss Greer), a few contestants went so far as to do some original research. Miss Myrtle Beach gives the tourism industry a valuable insight when she lists South Carolina's greatest attractions as "sun, beaches, and proximity to the ocean," the latter always a plus when beaches are involved (Gaston being a possible exception). And Miss Charleston points out that, although "according to research, one does not necessarily die from drinking anti-freeze," it should never be served with fish.

The highlight was Miss Barnwell's stark essay simply entitled "Extintion" (sic), a guttural cry of the post-cold-war angst permeating our culture after 50 years on the brink of Apocalyptic destruction.

With only a handful of spelling errors.

It is a tragedy that only one of these women can be crowned on that fateful Saturday night. Some may mourn the brave but defeated contestants who must return to modeling classes or their reign as "Egg and Dairy Queen" (Miss Gaffney). But I say don't be sad. It is time for the naysayers and party poopers to realize, as Miss Wade Hampton-Taylors does, that "real beauty goes beyond the skin."

That's right. It goes all the way to the Sherman College of Straight Chiropractic.

November, 1993

23

BOWLED OVER

In December, 1994, the University of South Carolina Gamecocks and the West Virginia Mountaineers were invited to play in the Carquest Bowl. The Gamecocks won that game, their first bowl victory ever, by a score of 23-10. I couldn't believe it, either.--MG

It's the Bubba Bowl, the Hatfields and the McCocks, the Redneck Rumble in Miami's Urban Jungle, the Inbreeder's Cup, 1994!

Yes, it's West Virginia vs. South Carolina, the Barefooters versus the Book Burners, the Black Lungs against the Bible Belts, a battle royale between those monoliths of mediocrity, those pinnacles of perennial loserdom, the Gamecocks and the Mountaineers.

One can almost hear the sound of a marketing director's salary plummeting at Carquest Inc. as word of this Bumble of the Century reaches upper management. What ads do you run for the Carolina-West Virginia demographic?

"At Carquest, we'd love to service your car, IF IT WEREN'T SITTING ON BLOCKS IN YOUR DRIVEWAY!!"

Or, "It's Twofer Tuesday--Lube and oil your doublewide for half price!"

I am not much of a football fan, but the irony of these two teams, these "Bowl Brothers" meeting on the field of valor, is exquisitely delicious. It's mythology in the making.

Let's face it: these two universities aren't likely to meet in the "Quiz Bowl" championship or on Jeopardy's "Campus Challenge." Outside the National Tractor Pull or the USA Spittoon-Off, football is the only chance they have to compete. That's a shame, because the histories of these programs are identical paradigms of the incompetent pursuit of athletic excellence.

For example, before Carolina signed on as the new doormat of the Southeastern Conference, both teams were independents. Like West Virginia, Carolina used to pack its schedule with powerhouses such as Miami (of Ohio) and Virginia (Barber College) in a cynical attempt to steal a National Title. Carolina eventually gave up, but West Virginia almost pulled the con. In 1993, the Mountaineers went to the Sugar Bowl and came within a mere 102 points of beating a real school, which would have made them national champs and scientifically proven the need for an NCAA football play-off system.

Other similarities between USC and UWV include: their commitment to academic excellence (both schools recruit heavily in Mississippi in an attempt to raise their own test scores); pampering new head coaches, who often keep their jobs long enough to pay off a VCR from Acme Rent-to-Own; and their anachronistically-correct mascots, one of which is a stupid, mean-spirited yard bird whose once-prized combat is now illegal, and the other a symbol of the Appalachian social pathologies that made "Deliverance" a believable film.

As they prepare to do battle, the question is begged: "What's the point?" If South Carolina beats West Virginia, so what? What did you do, coach? Throw them off by asking their linemen to count to an even number on their fingers? And if the Mountaineers win, what of it? Carolina has never, ever won a bowl game. St. Mary's School for Girls would beat the "Chokin' Chickens" if the game is on national TV.

Given the traditions of these schools, I'm beginning to wonder if there can actually be a winner. I fully expect them to play to a scoreless tie, and, through a little-known quirk in the rules, have the game stricken from the record books when, after four quarters, neither team has a first down.

Having said that, I'd love to go to Miami for the game, just to see the faces of the Hispanic "Home Boys" when Jed Clampett and the Jeff Davis-mobile come rollin' into Little Havana one December weekend. Thousands of lily-white rednecks loose in Miami, last week's paycheck hanging out of their "Forget, Hell!" jacket pockets? It'll be a white Christmas, indeed.

"Don't shoot! Here's muh wallet--Hey, how could y'all tell we wuz from outta town?"

"I don't know, man, but could you tell the guy strapped to the hood to stop playin' that banjo..."

December, 1994

Chapter 2

CLINTON AND ME

Clinton and Me

Just over a year ago, in the same week William Jefferson Clinton was sworn in as head of our national family, I became a father. I'm not sure which one of us was more nervous, but I was probably photographed more than he was that week.

While the president stood in the chilling January wind and delivered his inaugural address, I paced a cold hospital floor with my newly-delivered son, Mencken. As the president prayed for wisdom and strength to lead our nation, I prayed, too. I prayed I wouldn't drop him, that the odor from his diaper was just gas, that he wouldn't grow up to appear on TV talk shows ("Psycho Killers and the Parents Who Raise Them--on the next Oprah.") .

Like President Clinton, most of the credit for my achievement must go to the dogged determination of my wife who, unbeknownst to me, was promoting my rise to fatherhood by secretly dumping her birth-control products into the toilet.

Behind every great man...

And, like the president, I was an unlikely nominee for my leadership position. I had no previous experience, and I was hardly the

27

consensus candidate of my wife's family. Then there was the character issue--I have none. I am notoriously irresponsible, immature and negligent. I once had a Chia Pet taken into protective custody by the SPCA.

Worse, I have a lifelong dislike of children. I have always found their noises, their sounds, their very presence, unbearable. "Children," I often noted, "should be *steamed*, not heard. And served with drawn butter."

Were it not for my innate "Bobbittophobia," I would have had a vasectomy long ago.

A poll of friends and family would have put the odds of my being a father on par with Michael Jackson being named spokesman for Underoos, or of an unknown Arkansas politico with an aversion to military service and a taste for coed slumber parties becoming Commander-In-Chief.

In our first year, President Clinton and I have approached the daunting tasks at hand with enthusiasm, if not competence. While the White House struggled to put together a cabinet, I discovered I had an ex-officio child-rearing "cabinet" consisting of every female relative and/or co-worker my wife has ever known. While the president was distancing himself from Zoe Baird and Kimba Wood, I was trying to figure out how to get their tax-free nannies to move to South Carolina. And as the president signed the "Family Leave Bill," guaranteeing all loving parents the right to stay home with their newborns, my wife was screaming, "If you think I'm gonna be trapped in this house with that 20 decibel drool machine, you're out of your mind!"

As the president's poll numbers dropped, so did my confidence. Maybe I wasn't the right man for the job. With household deficits rising due to the sudden surge in spending by the "Dept. of Diapers and Bizarre Rash Ointments," I barely managed to squeak through my budget proposal. Victory was assured only after a hefty increase in the "Anyone Who Has Worn The Same Smock For 9 Months Deserves All The New Clothes She Wants" Fund.

Somehow we stumbled forward. Through the hot summer and the fading fall, the president and I refused to quit. Sure, there were embarrassing moments for both of us--fortunately, I don't have any

Janet "Fireball" Reno's or Ron "Ho Chi Minh" Brown's to answer for. President Clinton got NAFTA and I got Mencken to sleep through the night, and we both had to wrestle a goofy-looking whiner with big ears to do it. Then came GATT and big jump in fourth-quarter growth and drinking from a cup and my first solo baby bath (no fatalities). It looks like things may be turning around.

Are they? Who knows. The economy and children are both very resilient. It could be that they would flourish with or without our guidance. They are also very fickle, and the healthy growth of a well-fed youngster can quickly turn into the pitiful cry of a croupy child. We can only hope for the best.

So happy birthday, Mencken Graham, and congratulations on your first year, Mr. President. I was with you all the way.

Oh, and have you heard about the terrible twos?

January, 1994

DON'T JUMP!

When Bob Franklin arrived at his business office the morning after the 1992 presidential election, he was surprised when his office manager, a previously placid young lady, stormed into work demanding to be paid in gold bouillon "until that draft-dodging Democrat gets the boot!" Later, he found her on the ledge outside her fifth-story office, holding a broom handle like a rifle and pointing it at passing cars. "She seemed to be saying something about Sirhan Sirhan, but it was hard to tell," Mr. Franklin told rescue workers as they escorted the young woman home.

A South Carolina woman called the highway patrol late Tuesday night to report her husband missing since early that evening. "We were watching the news, and when they said Georgia had gone for Clinton, he just disappeared," the woman told police. A stable family man and staunch Republican, he was eventually found wandering northward along I-95 wearing only an "Annoy the Media, Re-Elect Bush" bumper sticker. He told officers he was "headed to Canada," and that his clothes had "been taxed off my back by Bill Clinton."

The walking wounded of the Republican Party are all around us. Despondent country clubbers trudge slowly down the fairway, their tee shots listless and unsteady. Stay-at-home moms forget to pick up children from soccer practice. Business owners stockpile canned food and copies of *The National Review* in their basements. The only spark of life comes at noontime, when Rush Limbaugh crackles from their AM radios, but each day the expected announcement--Clinton's victory was actually a fraud perpetrated by the GLM (Godless Liberal Media) and late results from Hawaii give the edge to President Bush--fails to arrive.

For political realists, the shock is hard to understand. A Clinton victory had been looming for months, a metaphysical certainty since the debates. The only Republican plan that offered any hope was the "Sherman Strategy," in which George Bush promised that, if elected, he would refuse to serve.

Still, many of our Republican friends and loved ones are on the verge of doing something drastic: slashing their wrists, moving to Guam, wearing a "Vote Helms!" T-Shirt into a gay biker bar. What can you do to help? Here are a few talking points that could save a Republican life:

Be positive. Yes, we lost a Republican president, but hey--it was George Bush! He was a lousy Republican anyway. Tax hikes, quota bills, a complete inability to master the English language. What's the big deal? It's not like we lost Reagan.

Look to the future. As long as Bush was in office, there loomed the terrifying prospect of a Quayle/Schwartznegger ticket in 1996. A Quayle-led ticket would do for Republicans what Millard Fillmore did for the "Know Nothing" Party in 1856. Thanks to the Bush beating, Dan Quayle will be selling shoes in Terre Haute and the field will be clear for winnable Republicans such as Bob Dole, Phil Gramm and (dare I say?) Carroll Campbell.

Look at the big picture. Remember: Bill Clinton was only elected president; it's not like he can really <u>do</u> anything. Now, if he had become guest host for Larry King, or was named chairman of the House Ways and Means committee--you know, if he really had some power--then I'd be worried. But he's only the president. So, until you see him photographed with Madonna or broadcasting his own radio talk show, relax. And after Sam Donaldson, Dick Gephart, the NRA, NOW, AARP and the ABRF (Arkansas Bimbo's Retirement Fund) do their jobs, you'll hardly recognize him at all.

Read your history. Remember when Reagan was elected and limp-wristed leftists ran screaming into their art-deco bomb shelters, certain the right-wing warmonger would push the red button half-an-hour after taking the oath. Instead, he ended the Cold War, brought democracy to Central America and kept defense spending under 7 percent of GNP.

Similarly, Republicans are traumatized because they started believing their own campaign ads. Yes, Bill Clinton is a draft-dodger, a known liar and an adulterer. But he's also a politician who wants to win again. He has no vested interest in hurting America, no secret plan to destroy capitalism and institute a liberal Goddess-worshipping theocracy.

The American Republic has made it through Supply-Side (Reagan and Bush), Tax and Spend (Johnson and Bush) and Slip and Fall (Gerald Ford). I am confident we will survive a little Sex and Gore.

So no more tears: You've got four years of Clinton and Congress-bashing ahead, and you should enjoy them while you can. If President Clinton keeps his promise to do for America what he did for Arkansas, there could be a Republican electoral lock before he finishes his first year.

November, 1992

BUREAUBUBBA

A friend told me a story: She had taken a day off work to attend to some personal business and spend time with her four-year-old daughter. About midday, she received a notice from the city: "Dear Sucker, er...Taxpayer--we are cutting off your water in two days for failure to pay your bill. If you come downtown and complain, we'll just give you a parking ticket. Love, City Hall."

My fastidious friend had already paid her bill, but she dutifully got on the phone and, after having her call passed around like a bad cold, was told she would have to produce her last two water payment checks. She had one, but the other, for $18, was with the bank, which would happily charge her $12 for a photocopy of the $18 check.

She took the checks to the city and worked her way through the bureaucratic maze, eventually ending up in a shouting match with Aunt Esther (of *Sanford and Son* fame) before convincing the city to clear up its mistake. The end result? The city begrudgingly allowed her to continue bathing while she lost an entire day of her life because a bureaucrat in City Hall can't read.

While City Hall bureaucrats are a nuisance, they are rarely dangerous. Admittedly, it's an inconvenience having a mayor who thinks "job growth" is something you have removed with laser surgery, but it's hardly a threat to personal security. As a society, we have a healthy disrespect for civil servants who, by the way, offer few useful services and are rarely civil. Bureaucrats, like roaches, may be impossible to eradicate, but we tolerate them by avoiding them when possible and giving them plenty of paid holidays.

And we NEVER let them have guns.

That is the reason, I believe, that Americans don't trust the United Nations.

President Clinton does not share this distrust. Indeed, this is why America's Bosnia "policy" (for lack of a better word) is a failure; in his heart and soul, President Clinton believes in the power of position papers and summit meetings to make a better world. The primary cause of human suffering, President BureauBubba believes, is the inability to fill out the right form.

It made sense to him, then, when the Serbs, Muslims and Croats of Yugoslavia re-opened a 500-year blood feud, to leave the matter in the hands of the UN, the most powerful bureaucratic machine in the world, other than the student loan system.

The UN is a bureaucrat's dream come true. It has a huge government, but no country. It has a huge budget but no constituents. Its headquarters is a palatial office where everyone is a Deputy, no one is in charge, and every floor speaks a different language. Imagine your local school board with a Belgian accent, and you've got the picture.

And they have the world's first bureaucratic army. It *looks* like an army, anyway, though the UN forces in Bosnia act more as a group of easy-to-spot hostages in matching outfits.

When the war began, the Bosnian government held well over a third of the territory and was prepared to defend itself to the death. In 1993, the UN's head BureauGeek, Butrous-Butrous Ghali (even his name is redundant!) sent in the "Peacekeepers" to protect the rights of Bosnian Muslims to be starved, beaten and raped within the allowable limits of the Geneva convention. Today, Bosnia's territory has been reduced to a handful of mobile home parks scattered across the mountains.

The United Nations also imposed an arms embargo to prevent the disarmed Bosnians from shooting back at the well-armed Serbs (kind of like a Brady Bill for tanks). "You don't need guns," President Clinton and our UN allies told the Bosnians; "we're here to protect you....By the way, you wanna buy a used car?"

The high point of our bureaucratic bungling came when an elected Bosnian leader was dragged from his UN-escorted car by a group of Serbs and executed in the presence of the UN "soldiers." The soldiers claimed that they would have gladly rescued the Bosnian from these Serb murderers if only he had presented the required two photo IDs.

That's the definition of a UN Security Force. When other people start shooting at you, their job is to take away your gun.

Even more pathetic have been the Clinton administration's attempts at pro-UN P.R. Newscasts begin with footage of whole towns destroyed, accounts of mass rape and executions, but end with dour-faced white guys in the Clinton Administration delivering straight lines such as "We are gravely concerned....We are considering action...this situation is serious..."

Boing! Calling the captain of the Titanic: Looks like you're having a little trouble with your boat....

Piling tragedy on tragedy is the fact that this genocidal mess was completely unnecessary. The nation of Yugoslavia was never a true nation. Since the late 1800's its penciled-in borders have been drawn by bureaucrats, most recently the Communists. When the Evil Empire fell and that bureaucracy collapsed, war between the Serbs, Croats and Muslims was inevitable.

That inevitable war of 1993 could have been swift, self-contained, and over by Christmas. Instead, a new set of bureaucrats have intervened (ours) and, in a good-hearted attempt to avoid the unavoidable, we have brought Bosnia years of unnecessary torture, rape and death.

Amazingly, the Bosnian fiasco has not shaken President BureauBubba's confidence in government. The current occupants of the White House still believe that a government health board can make us well, a government tax plan can make us prosperous and a civil service fight force can bring peace to the world.

Meanwhile, be sure to pay your water bill. Or else.

July, 1995

EVERY AMERICAN'S RIGHT

The following is an excerpt from President Clinton's 1997 State of the Union address, following his narrow electoral college victory over the Limbaugh/Thurmond ticket.--MG.

My fellow citizens, you have sent me back to Washington to continue the work of bringing true security to our nation, and I am ready.

We began in 1994 by bringing health security to every American. Our universal health care program brought equity and access to all. While the overall program is a little more expensive than the $2 trillion dollars we estimated, I pleased to announce that costs are dropping somewhat this year, due to a drastic increase in the number of people who died while waiting to see a doctor. Nevertheless, we brought you health security. *[Congress applauds]*

I admit, the civil disturbances that came with the small, 20 percent rise in income taxes caught me by surprise, but instead of focusing on the challenges, I seized the opportunity. We used the civil war of 1995 to confiscate every legally-held weapon in America, our first step in crime security. And Surgeon General Elders announced today that, thanks to the national disarming, fewer criminals are being shot while committing crimes. The result is yet another health care savings. *[Congress applauds, camera zooms on Joycelyn Elders smoking a joint]*

Then we took a tremendous step forward in social justice by guaranteeing every person access to a job--true job security. This law, which gives jobseekers the right to sue employers who don't hire them, has created a dramatic increase in the number of job applications, as well as a surge in the number of trial lawyers. These aren't minimum wage jobs, either. Lawyers make big money--when they don't get caught. Isn't that right, Hillary. *[Laughter, camera pan of Hillary and her parole officer in balcony]*

After guaranteeing every American a job, we discovered that some Americans didn't make as much money as others because of differences in education. A student who could get into Harvard made more money than one who went to tech school. So we passed a law making every college and university in America charge the same price. Immediately, the cost of tech school jumped to $20,000 a year. Hey, no one said the security would be cheap.

That is the record of the first four years of my administration, and it is a record to be proud of: health security, crime security, job and education security. Now it is time to face the single greatest challenge facing working Americans today: Auto Care.

Millions of Americans lack access to quality auto repair and insurance. They can't afford the premiums, the coverage and the warranties that wealthier drivers take for granted. When the working poor have a fender bender, or need emergency care--an alternator transplant, an expensive overhaul--they can be plunged into debt or, worse, lose their cars altogether.

Without access to affordable auto repair service, Americans cannot get to their jobs, to their churches, or--I want to remind all you incumbent Congressmen--to the polls. It is clearly in our...er, America's best interest to have the government guarantee quality car care for our citizens. *[Loud cheers from Congress, close up of new Auto Care Czar, Richard Petty]*

My plan is simple. Every American pays one price to the statewide "Auto Service Board," regardless of the car they drive or their driving record. After all, my national health plan didn't differentiate between healthy people and unhealthy people. If smokers and non-smokers, joggers and non-joggers, sky divers and non-skydivers pay the same price for health insurance, shouldn't speeders and non-speeders pay the same price for auto insurance?

And, just as with my health care plan, no one can opt out. Every driver must buy their auto insurance from the government. And, just like health insurance, selling private auto insurance will be illegal. Why should someone else be able to buy insurance that you can't afford, just because they have earned more money? I ask you, is that the American way?

And finally, since the major cost of auto insurance is in repairing expensive, luxury cars, these cars will no longer be manufactured or sold in the United States. Americans who drive Caddys and Porsches will pay the same car payment they do today, but these drivers will be issued Ford Escorts just like the rest of us. At last, we will have true equity on the highways. *[Standing ovation]*

I know what our right-wing radical opponents will say. They will say that the reason some people have nicer cars and better insurance is because these individuals worked harder in school, or excelled in business, or avoided bad choices in life. Some heartless conservatives actually believe that the few in our society who produce more *deserve* a better life. *[boos from balcony, close up of Newt Gingrich eating raw beef with his bare hands]*

Well, I say that every American deserves a better life whether he earns it or not!

I say that, if you are an American, you deserve the best health care, the best economic care and the best car care regardless of your personal actions, abilities or decisions. And whether you're driving a Yugo or a Jaguar, if you stick with me, we will all be in the same boat.

May the Mother Goddess bless you, and Mother Goddess Bless America! *[Shouts of hosanna; Clinton is whisked off to awaiting sorority party]*

February, 1994

LET US PRAY

Thanksgiving is here, a time when even the most callous and materialistic among us pause to consider what might be on the mind of the big You-Know-Who in the Sky.

It is standard greeting-card mythology that, on Thanksgiving, we Americans express humble gratitude for three squares a day and the roof over our heads. Actually, the few introspective moments Americans spend each Thanksgiving are dominated, not by gratitude for our meager successes, but spiritual sighs of relief for disasters avoided.

When the roast turkey is set before us, many Americans will glance at the dead bird and whisper, "There but for the grace of God and a faulty Breathalizer go I." "How horribly tragic my life might have been," we ponder, "if my boss had ever audited my expense account, if my Trig professor hadn't graded on the curve, if Gail Stewart's rabbit had died after prom night...."

As the infallible Mencken noted, "Anyone can bear injustice; what stings is justice."

And so, on Thanksgiving, we take a moment to thank the Almighty for His most precious blessing, justice denied.

This is the motive to which I ascribe Speaker-Presumptive Newt Gingrich's call for a constitutional amendment allowing prayer in schools. Though school prayer is not part of the infamous "Contract With (Normal) America," it has been a touchstone of Gingrich's post-election activity.

Why? I imagine a fervent, late-night "Deal with God," a prayer by the desperate would-be Speaker of the House on the eve of the elections: "Lord, if you'll just let Clinton campaign publicly for a few more days--without getting shot or divorced--I'll get you school prayer, an end to tax-funded abortions, and I'll stop calling Pat Robertson 'Elmer Gaptooth,' I promise!"

Some attribute Newt's school prayer plan to partisan politics: Prayer in schools is extremely popular, especially during exam week, and opposing it is dangerous for Democrats. Democrats cannot afford to become the Anti-God party, especially now that they have firmly established themselves as the Anti-Business Party, the Anti-Military Party and Anti-Victory Party party.

With their ranks decimated, their president in peril, their policies abandoned, and facing the Republican steamroller of God, Gingrich and Capital Gains, all the Democrats can do is pray.

And they are. In fact, my spies inside the Democrat National Committee have obtained a copy of the Democrat Party's official Thanksgiving Day prayer, prepared by staff attorneys with the Congressional Office of Metaphysics and Spiritual Subsidization:

"Dear, God, I need this job--PLEASE, God, I'm begging, let me keep this job and get Hillary off my back, that b... "

Oops, that's an unreleased copy of the *White House* Thanksgiving Day prayer. Here is the Democrats' Thanksgiving Day Prayer:

"O Great Eternal Force, Thou All-Powerful, All-Knowing (Yet Open to Reasoned Debate on All Issues), Non-Judgmental, Gender-Neutral Entity of the Universe, We approach You this day in the spirit of cooperation and bipartisan compromise, thanking You for the many bountiful gifts to which we are entitled under federal law (penalties for failing to provide said 'gifts' found under Title IX, 'Bountiful Entitlements Act').

We acknowledge our shortcomings--though we oppose any standardized method of measuring achievement, as such methods might be biased against the 'morally challenged'--and we pray for Your forgiveness. [Counsel's Note: This plea for forgiveness should not be construed as an admission of guilt, nor any claim of liability for acts covered by this plea.]

As we gather for our first Thanksgiving under Republican rule, we ask You to give us generous hearts, to bear no resentment against the right-wing Nazi extremists who have corrupted our national political system, or the fascist radio talk show hosts who have poisoned America's mind against us. We pray that You will bless the GOP in their earnest efforts to destroy the economy and install a dictatorial Theocracy, and we pray that their efforts will bring our Republican counterparts their just reward. [Counsel's Note: All references to "hellfire" and/or "eternal damnation" were struck by Sen. Kennedy in committee.]

We are all the Inner Children of God. [Waving healing crystals at this time is optional.] *We have a firm commitment to the overall goals of the Ten Commandments, though we continue to disagree on their implementation. Just as the children of Israel were delivered from Egypt by Your hand--through bilateral negotiations supported by Democratic administrations--so we pray that You will deliver us back to our rightful place as Your faithful servants in the public sector.*

Bless this vegetarian meal before us, and keep us ever mindful of the unionized labor and agriculture subsidies which made it possible. We pray/meditate in the name of our various deities, goddesses and/or self-actualized spiritual forces within...." Amen.

November, 1994

CLINTON AND ME, TWO

Two years ago last week, the same week William Jefferson Clinton was sworn in as head of our national family, I became a father. This time last year, I wrote a column, "Clinton and Me," in which I noted the frightening similarities between the president and me in our enthusiastic but inept efforts to assume the duties of our new offices. I ended my article with a lighthearted reference to "the terrible twos."

Ha, ha.

Patterning his behavior after the cantankerous 103rd Congress, my son Mencken took it upon himself to prove that the "terrible" part arrives well before the second birthday. Sure, we got off to a good start. Like the president, I had "The Big MO" coming into the new year, and I thought 1994 was going to be pretty good. The "Comeback Kid" had health care all but wrapped up in Washington, while my wife, Jennifer, and I had agreed on a socially-progressive budget, with heavy subsidization of such vital programs as the "Tanning Salon Supplement" and "Aid to Moms Who Might Eat Their Young if You Don't Get a Sitter Friday Night."

My wife and I also had consensus on the divisive social issue of child discipline. Unfortunately, our plan resembled the Clinton health care plan in that it worked great until you actually used it. When, for example, Mencken discovered his ability to "express himself" through the destruction of property and unorthodox distribution of bodily wastes (we suspect he received NEA funding), Jennifer and I were completely unprepared. She suddenly revealed a hidden liberal agenda, fighting my efforts at discipline and insisting on being called Jennifer

Rodham Graham. Meanwhile, I clung to my more conservative principles and advocated a Singaporean model of social justice. I wanted to beat the kid's brains in.

This division in our leadership left an opening for Mencken who, like the House Republicans, was a master of exploiting weakness. When I discovered him standing over the commode holding the cord of my electric razor (the rest had been roto-rootered), he rushed to the sympathetic arms of his mother. When he sensed she was on the verge of violence, he whipped up a few crocodile tears and clung to my leg. It was transparent political rhetoric, but somehow I couldn't resist. It was Gerber Gridlock, pure and simple.

Eventually, it became clear that my son considered my commands mere "suggestions," and not particularly worthwhile suggestions at that. If I said "Put it down," he picked it up. If I said "Go left," he went right. My administration was rudderless, drifting. My message wasn't penetrating.

Everyone had suggestions as to how we should repair our damaged public image, though we never went as far as President Clinton, who invited a psychic and a motivational speaker to the White House. I was urged by my father to govern from the Right ("Spare the rod and spoil the child! You got to beat some sense into 'em!"). My mother counseled a more liberal approach ("He's just a baby, he didn't mean to hurt anyone. Besides, you can always get another cat..").

Then came the disastrous fall. Kooks were shooting at the White House, and I was robbed at gunpoint in my driveway. Our poll numbers were plummeting, our wives were on the warpath, and just when it seemed it couldn't get any worse...Whammo! a chubby-cheeked interloper suddenly stole the limelight and began pushing a radical program of self-promotion.

Newt, meet Alex.

Actually, it's Alexandra. For the second time in less than 20 months, my wife and I had a baby.

And talk about hogging the camera! Like Speaker Gingrich, little Alex can't belch without making headlines. I'm trying to get the family focused on long-term issues (like the need for my wife to be sterilized);

instead, the baby-hungry paparazzi spend all day with their heads in the crib, observing every move of the new House leader.

In fact, listening to the president's pleading tones this past year, I heard a frighteningly familiar sound: the whining voice of a man realizing that no one is paying any attention to what he is saying. Our vocabulary in this, our second year of parenthood, has consisted largely of sighs of frustrations and occasional bursts of anger. Meanwhile, no one was listening.

Well, Mr. President, no one said this would be easy. And, in fact, there have been some fun moments...well, for me, anyway. I have heard it said that being president is the most demanding, frustrating, punishing job in the world, that every president eventually leaves office feeling they were abused, unappreciated and generally worn plumb out. Yet every former president agrees that it was the most rewarding part of their public careers.

After two years as a father, I know the feeling. Happy Birthday, Mencken, and good luck Mr. President. We're going to need it.

January, 1995

Chapter 3

GUYS AND DOLLS

GET ME TO THE CHURCH
ON TIME

I just spent six months being lied to, yelled at, threatened, dressed up, shaken down and, finally, publicly humiliated.

No, I didn't run for public office.

Worse.

I got married.

Now, don't start pushing me for details about the ceremony. I was lucky I made it to the right church on the right day. It amazes me when people (read: women) start asking me what color the bridesmaids wore. I was just the groom; I'm not absolutely certain what color the *bride* was wearing. As soon as I entered the church, I fell into a condition commonly diagnosed as the Wedding Coma, a form of mental paralysis that afflicts men until they have bags of birdseed hurled at their crania.

My wedding music? Don't remember a note. The vows? For men, the entire ceremony consists of vague muttering along the lines of "mumble, mumble...PRISON!...mumble, mumble...ENTRAPMENT! mumble...OWNING A STATION WAGON FOR THE REST OF MY LIFE!"

I do not claim to speak for women. It may have been just as disconcerting for my wife to enter holy matrimony as it was for me. But watching the condescending smiles and constant licking of chops by women at weddings leads me to believe otherwise.

There is something disingenuous about the way women approach weddings. That's what I object to: the pretense that any part of this obscene spectacle at hand is inherently reasonable.

To put it politely: Yank, yank.

If the point of the wedding ceremony were marriage, it would be a five-minute event featuring a judge and stern warnings about joint bank accounts. If it were about celebrating, it would be a dressy toga party with bad lounge acts.

Instead, weddings are pretentious displays of wealth and class, inspired by the fear of uncertain social status. They are an embarrassing throwback to days when daughters were economic encumbrances that were (in sales jargon) "difficult to move." Closing the deal often involved large factory-to-dealer incentives, not to mention liberal doses of grain alcohol and, if necessary, a whiff of buckshot.

This social anachronism, the wedding, seems a perfect target in this day of militant P.C. paranoia, and one would suppose they would be on the decline. One would be terribly mistaken. The wedding industry is booming, capable of sustaining hundreds of monthly bridal publications, each the size of the Atlanta phone book, and all containing the same five articles.

The article that represents the perihelion of pre-wedding hypocrisy is entitled: "Weddings on a Budget." Nestled as it is between full-page photos of $10,000 wedding gowns and diamonds the size of grapefruit, the article fails to make a convincing argument for frugality. Indeed, the writer (usually a woman with several hyphens in her name) seems to disdain her own suggestions:

"If you're trying to stay in a budget, you could always rent or borrow a dress, I suppose...that is, if your father is the kind of cheap, selfish, WRETCHED BEAST WHO WOULD FORCE HIS OWN CHILDREN TO WALK BAREFOOT THROUGH THE SNOW!"

The first lie a man will hear after handing over the zirconia is: "I don't want a fancy wedding." The second? "And I want you to be involved." After that, it's all downhill.

Upon engagement, any young lady who cares about her victim,...er, fiancé should set him down and lovingly tell him: "Look, chump! Between now and the wedding day, you're excess baggage. You're just going to get in the way. Just make sure the tux fits and then get lost until I need you. And don't get any bright ideas about backing out, because either way, I KEEP THE RING."

Don't get me wrong: Weddings can be beautiful bonding experiences, bringing two people who love each other closer than they've ever been before. Unfortunately for the groom, those two people are the bride and her mother. Mother and daughter have been known to disappear for month at a time just before the wedding, apparently beamed away to a distant planet entirely inhabited by beings who can listen to your bride-to-be prattle on for hours about angel's breath without once sneaking a peak at the Braves game over her shoulder, sending her into tearful hysterics about canceling the wedding and flinging herself from an overpass.

Let's face it, guys. We can't win. Perhaps that's what weddings are truly about: a show of force, a clear demonstration of who is really in charge. Looked at from the male point of view, our wedding week is a lot like hell week for a particularly sadistic fraternity. Every event is designed to make us sweaty, uncomfortable and self-conscious. Any shred of male ego we may have nurtured through the ceremony, any hope for a future free from female dominance is lost when we see who has to write the wedding-day check:

Dear old Dad.

June, 1992

45

A WOMAN'S PLACE

An Actual Letter From a Recent Women's Magazine:

"A reader complained that your magazine had changed from an informative, professional magazine to a women's Playboy. Evidently she is WAY behind the times, expecting that reader's interests are the same as they were a decade ago. I thoroughly enjoy the magazine, and I WANT, NEED and ENJOY reading about sex! I certainly agree with you that sex is a NATURAL part of women's lives. MORE SEX, PLEASE!"
Signed, Name Withheld by Request.

I want to state, for the record, that my wife is mostly sane. That she is an avid reader of what are euphemistically called "women's magazines" should not discount her overall value as a human being, any more than the fact that I own every Queen album ever released means that I have absolutely no taste in music.

We all have our little quirks.

Since our marriage I've glanced at quite a few of these ladies' journals and gotten a taste of their feminist flavor. I usually read them when I'm stuck in the household "library," where a stack is always handy. Like many men in that situation, I begin my reading with the mousse and hairspray canisters (not much plot development, but I enjoy the tight, punchy prose!)

Then a Cosmo headline will catch my eye, usually something like "10 Hot Sex Tips" or "Women's True Stories of Ecstasy" or "Women Who Really Love Sex--I Mean, These Women Think It's Fantastic, Honest! They Never Have Headaches, Really!" I quickly flip to these promising pieces, which always have a steamy photo and hot lead: "Sonja never thought of herself as kinky, until she met Sven...." How disappointing to read on and discover that Sven's idea of "kinky" is to spend all night snuggling and listening to Manilow albums, then, upon waking the next morning, lifting Sonja into his arms and saying: "Yes,

I could cover you with whipped topping and make mad passionate love to you, but what I really want to do is take you to...the MALL!"

Speaking for men everywhere, this isn't "kinky"--it's perverse.

I'm beginning to believe the publishers of women's magazines know men are reading these "sex tips" articles, and they are intentionally using them to mock us. I recently snatched up a magazine with the cover story: "10 Things Every Woman Loves To Hear In Bed, Guaranteed to Make Her Sit Up And Beg!" I turn the page and it reads: "HA! You think we're going to tell YOU that?!"

These so-called "women's magazines" are, in fact "girlie magazines" in the truest sense. Every little girl with a curl and a lobotomy can enjoy them without guilt, but for any thinking person-- with or without a uterus--they are insulting.

Women's magazines are almost single-minded in their schizophrenia. They regularly feature covers with contradictory headlines. "Learn To Love Your Age" is inevitably paired with "Look 10 Years Younger--The Latest Research." "Build Your Body Confidence" has a companion story "Swimsuits that Slim You."

The message of women's magazines is clear: "Love yourself just as you are--as long as you're like Cindy Crawford. As a woman, you are more than just an object to be ogled. You are a well-informed, well-adjusted, thoroughly cosmetitized and over-dressed object to be ogled, and don't you forget it, Helen Gurley America!"

Now, before you pick up your Ladysmith .357 and drive over to my house (See *Cosmo's* "Men, Magnums and Mousse: Hairstyle Safety Tips for Well-Armed Woman") let me point out that I am NOT saying that women who read these magazines are dumber than men. I am simply saying that they are dumb. Stupid is a gender-neutral affliction, and the billion-dollar men's magazine industry, from Playboy to "Katrina's Kinky Kennell," proves it.

More to the point, I believe men's (read: "girlie") magazines and women's (read: "girlie") magazines have quite a bit in common. They both feature artificially-enhanced women in bizarre situations: A model, her hair perfect as she jumps out of an airplane for *Glamour*; a porno queen, hair perfect as she rides a llama into a hot tub for *Wanker Weekly*. Both genres define a woman by the current state of her body, and by her willingness to let men judge her value by that standard. And both magazines rely on a great deal of airbrushing.

The cover of one recent mag read: "How Intelligent Women Flirt." Just a hint, ladies. If you have to buy a magazine to find out, don't bother.

April, 1994

KNOCK ON WOODY

Remember the good old days when the mention of Woody Allen's latest film at a dinner party would immediately divide the room into the "Hip" and the "Clueless"? Especially in the South, where the question, "Do you like Woody Allen?" is frequently answered: "You bet! He's my favorite person on 'Cheers'!"

Well, don't try it now. At a recent gathering of Carolina cognoscenti, I made the mistake of asking a group of women if they had seen Woody Allen's *Husbands and Wives*.

I had to throw them raw beef to keep them at bay.

"I think it's terrible," replied a young woman in a Malcolm X T-shirt.

Wait a minute. You think *Husbands and Wives* was terrible?

"I think *he's* terrible," she said.

But have you seen the film? I was wondering what you thought of the movie.

"I don't know if I want to give him any of my money," sneered another woman, her herbal-tea liberalism dripping from every word.

Well, I had seen the film, and I thought it was excellent. As for the scandal, it has turned into a boon for Woody Allen fans in the deep South by getting the film released here in the same decade it was produced. Considering we are still waiting for *Annie Hall* to hit town, I have nothing to complain about.

"He's such a pig," said another woman. "My God, it's incest after all."

Ignoring the irony of hearing incest decried in South Carolina, the heart of "Kissing Cousins" country, I commented that Woody and his heart throb, Soon-Yi, aren't related.

"Oh, you would say that," the herbal-tea liberal growled. "Men! You're all perverts! You all think it's OK for an old man to start dating some sweet young thing."

My head began to swim. A year ago this liberal die-hard was adamantly defending Robert Mapplethorpe and the right to inter-species conjugal relations (assuming consent on the part of the livestock). Suddenly she was ready to criminalize gold-digging and vanity?

Then again, she was right about one thing: Men are perverts, at least all the ones I know. It's easy to imagine, for example, a lost episode of the Brady Bunch in which Greg turns to Marsha and says: "You know, we aren't really brother and sister...."

Beyond the tasteless incest jokes, however, there was another point to be made, and before these women offered me as a human sacrifice to the Earth Goddess, I tried to make it.

"I'm not talking about Woody Allen as a person," I said, "I'm talking about the movie."

"Well, I saw the movie, and I feel sorry for Mia," replied the Malcolm X T-shirt. "I mean, Woody made her look so...so manipulating. He did it on purpose."

A woman? Manipulating? Hard to imagine, I know, but isn't it at least possible that she was just playing a part? You know, like in a *movie*?

"He's disgusting. I'll never go to another Woody Allen film, and I don't care what it's about."

Wait a minute. Now we've hit the wall.

I don't know much about Woody Allen's personal life other than the fact that, up until now, his relationships have all involved thin, squeaky, slightly neurotic women. And I don't really care about his personal life. He's an artist: I pay to see his art.

I'm not asking Woody to be my priest or rabbi. I'm not asking him for marriage counseling or a "12 Steps Toward Nebbishdom" program. I just want him to make films that are worth the $6.00 I pay to see them. And, *Shadows and Fog* aside, he's done a fine job.

When the Christian Coalition or CADRE (Citizens Adamantly Decrying Anything even Remotely Entertaining) line up outside local cinemas to protest *Ernest Saves Christmas* because Jim Varney passes gas in a manger scene, these protesters are mocked by the same people who are now condemning Allen's work without a viewing. If I stayed away from a film because the director was a homosexual, or a Communist, or had publicly called Ice-T "The Byron of Our Generation," I would be, in the eyes of these faux-liberals, a philistine. But when Volvo Vegetarian-types burn books because the author uses the adjective "beefy," they are doing the Lord's work.

My audience was unswayed. They muttered "Men!" several times, and shunned me for the rest of the evening, teaching me a valuable lesson.

Conservative or liberal, hip or square, black or white--women are always right.

January, 1993

I CAN'T GIVE YOU ANYTHING BUT LOVE

Valentine's Day approaches, and men across America are alternately annoyed and afraid: annoyed at the prospect of another woman-directed gift-giving holiday looming in our fiscal future (why isn't "Super Bowl Day" a holiday?), and afraid because we sense that this holiday involves a concept we don't understand: the art of the woo.

Wooing, the cause celebre of St. Valentine, is an art that has almost been entirely lost, mostly because men have stopped looking.

Woo, as every true artiste d'amour knows, is always "pitched"--never pursued, pressed or panted--reinforcing its gentleness. It is offered, a softball down the middle of the plate, and the receiver only has to hold out her bat. Wooing involves subtlety, shading and nuance, and is thus handled clumsily by the masculine breed, most of whom approach "love making" (I use the term in its original, more innocent sense) with the same sensitivity with which they change a flat tire: "I've got a job to do, I've got my tool right here, so let's get to it!"

Wooing is so passe that even the word is arcane, along with its counterparts "courting" and "petting." The latter, once a delightfully playful name for casual groping, has been virtually destroyed by its appearances in the phrase "heavy petting." This cumbersome label is, in turn, a product of earnest Evangelical "teen counselors" who, overcome by the blunt reality of teenage sexual activity, commandeered the word in a fit of euphemistic desperation, along with the phrases "deep kissing," "self abuse" and "until you go blind."

It is a shame that the Just Say No crowd hasn't made more progress, because the current rush to "do the nasty" has in many ways pushed aside the joy of the woo. While refraining from clichés involving cows, fences and the availability of lactose, there is truth in the notion that when sex arrives, courting dies.

Why? Because courting takes work, planning, resolve, and a level of concentration that men rarely achieve outside a football stadium. In matters of romance, it takes the prospect of "hitting a homer" to keep them swinging away at the plate.

This focus on accomplishment (the score) as opposed to process (the game) is a reason why men turn so often to sports analogies when discussing sex. Women understand the joy of the dance, the play, the game itself, while men myopically focus on putting points on the board.

Wooing is the art of playing. Sex is the ability to score.

That is why Valentine's Day is a perilous holiday for men, celebrating as it does the spontaneous joy of romance. If you want to see us at our worst, go to any card shop or flower store on the afternoon of Valentine's Day and watch the stream of grim, uninspired men pour in. We approach the work at hand with a sense of fiscal responsibility: "Hmm, can't get carnations--too cheap. How much for a dozen roses? What?! They were just 20 bucks a week ago! Oh, well, give me that bud vase with the 'Get Well Soon' card--I'll white it out later..."

The bounty is dutifully presented, the restaurant ritual is obediently performed, and if we are successful, we are given a feminine "pax vobiscum" and admonished to go and sin no more.

Yes, men do act spontaneously, especially early in relationships, but with mixed results. We lack a proper sense of whimsy, especially when it comes to gift-giving and event-coordinating. The gentleman who rushes in and cries enthusiastically "Grab your coat, Honey! I've got two tickets to "Chippendolls On Parade!" knows the feeling of getting it all wrong. Giving your loved one a new TV antenna or a week's worth of bowling--no matter how pragmatic--is hardly romancing the stone.

Valentine's Day is, at its core, a regimented exercise in romance, dictated by women to guarantee themselves at least one day in which men are forced to act like something besides men. What men need to do is seize the opportunity. Learn something. It's never too late.

So, gentlemen--do your duty. There is woo to be pitched, and as every good pitcher knows, the follow-through is everything.

February, 1994

BAD BOYS

As a young man, standing at the doorway of adulthood and hoping to encounter plenty of compliant women waiting on the other side, I was counseled by female friends to avoid being "too manly."

I was never much on "macho" to begin with (fear of personal injury kept me off the high school chess team), so I willingly took this advice. "Sensitivity" was the buzzword back in the late '70s and early '80s, when Donahue was hot and Alan Alda still played romantic leads. "I just want a man who'll make me laugh," women sighed breathlessly. "A sensitive man who writes poems, likes cats and really knows how to listen."

So I took these women to romantic nightspots (Ah, Denny's in the moonlight...) and spent all evening nodding understandingly and reciting Emily Dickinson Then, about the time things were supposed to get interesting, some redneck moron with a belt buckle the size of a hubcap would walk up to our table, pull the toothpick out of his mouth, point at the Firebird parked outside and say: "Hey, wench! How 'bout a good screw?"

Bam! She and Gomer are headed for the Mayberry Suites and I'm stuck with the check and a half-dozen pages of pathetic poetry. Thus, I learned an important lesson about dating: The same women who say they want sensitive, caring men who nurture their feminine nature will go home with Bubba if he has a nice butt.

Most women, that is. There are others, however, who are extremely unhappy about the state of contemporary manhood. These women are advocating sweeping changes in male conduct....and I'm not just talking about professional-tennis-playing women, either. There are some intelligent and serious-minded women who believe that the existence of the male sex is the greatest challenge facing the world today and, sensitive or not, it may be time to stock up the sperm banks and get rid of us all together.

One of these women is June Stephenson, a psychologist who wrote a book in 1992 entitled Men are Not Cost-Effective. This isn't one of those cute little truck-stop paperbacks that compare men to cucumbers or battery-operated appliances. It's a scholarly work that reviews cost-analysis data on crime, prisons, pollution, etc. and concludes that men are a luxury society simply cannot afford.

For example, though they are only half the population of America, men outnumber women in prison 94 to 6. Men commit the vast majority of crimes, costing society billions in lost property increased security costs and police efforts. Paying these costs falls equally upon men and women, Stephenson writes, and this is unfair: "Many women pay for male crime with their lives, but ALL women taxpayers pay for male crime with their tax dollars." Stephenson's solution to this inequity is an across-the-board $100 tax on every American member of the male sex.

That's right: A "Johnson" tax.

Actually, Stephenson uses the term "user fee," but this would exempt married men, so I don't think that's what she really means.

No, Stephenson is proposing a tax on our "manhood." She is calling on every red-blooded American male (other than John Wayne Bobbitt and Michael Jackson) to stand tall and do our duty. However, administering such a tax does give rise to problematic issues: Is a "flat tax" unfairly rigid? Shouldn't Jewish guys get a 20 percent reduction 7 days after their birth? What about men who have been surgically enlarged?

That certainly gives new meaning to a "Capital Gains" tax...

Perhaps the tax should be progressive, perhaps on a "per inch" basis, though this idea would no doubt meet with opposition in the African-American community. But progressivity has its advantages. No need for audits, for example, because every man in America is going to overpay. You can count on it.

If all this seems too silly to take seriously, you aren't a college professor or editorial writer (I first learned of Stephenson's book from a supportive newspaper editorial). Stephenson's fans defend the "penis proposal" as being similar to the common practice of forcing convicted criminals to pay restitution to crime victims.

However, there is one slight difference: Every criminal has committed some kind of actual crime, while there are men who have never done anything worse than leave the toilet seat up. Should they suffer, too?

"They're men, aren't they?" comes the feminists' answer. "Hangin's too good fer 'em!" All men are guilty because they're part of the same group, so the thesis goes. It's sort of the flip side of "group rights": group *wrongs*.

This is dangerous territory for Stephenson and her allies. A Stephenson-like analysis might reveal, for example, that black people are more likely to spend time in prison than other groups and therefore should pay a "black" tax. And is it fair that, while only women get pregnant, everyone's tax dollars are used to deliver babies in our public hospitals? How 'bout a womb tax?

For comprehensive revenue collection, what I propose is a "B&B" tax (Brains and...er, uh, "testicular fortitude"). That's the only fair tax on people like Ms. Stephenson and her allies who, though woefully underrepresented in the former, are generously endowed with the latter.

July, 1995

TIME OFF FOR GOOD BEHAVIOR

As you read this, perhaps as you grab a bite during a rushed lunch or impatiently wait in an office, I am on vacation. A summer, *family* vacation.

Pity me.

There is something perverse about the American theory of relaxation. Indeed, the words "relax" and "vacation" have precisely the same relationship as the phrases "good night's sleep" and "you will hang at dawn."

When I want to relax, I stop. Literally. I just stop doing and plop down in a chair, a hammock, a plate of food. Plop: instant relaxation. Where ever I am, it's a vacation.

When my wife Jennifer wants to relax, she goes. She goes out, away, anywhere. She packs, she prepares, she presses ever onward toward utopia. This year, utopia is in the mountains.

For my wife and I, choosing the mountains as our vacation destination was a compromise on the magnitude of the recent trade talks between the US and Japan. I was the Japanese, dragging my feet, slowing the process, hoping somehow we might make it through the entire summer without an agreement. Jennifer was Mickey Kantor, promising unspeakable retaliation if I didn't agree to something: a week at the beach, a week-end in Atlanta, a night at the Hooterville Hilton, we simply had to go *somewhere*.

We batted around a few ideas...actually, Jennifer did the swinging, I just pitched soft balls and watched them fly. She hated every vacation idea I offered, all of which were variations on the theme of staying home, doing nothing, eating out and sleeping late. This was in stark contrast to my wife, who insisted that a vacation isn't a vacation unless you're at an *expensive hotel*, doing nothing, eating out and sleeping late.

She finally coaxed me into the mountains by manipulating my two weaknesses: She knows I loathe the summer steambath that is South Carolina in August, and she knows I will participate in any activity offering even a remote possibility of sex.

(Note: for married men with two small children, sex is like a solar eclipse: extremely rare, and participation requires a lot of advanced planning.) So Jennifer had me when she proposed a vacation trip to a cool, mountain cabin in an area frequented by Hugh Grant.

But Jennifer got to pick the cabin. Being a man, I am insensitive to the requirements for adequate housing. I would ask rental agents stupid questions like: "How much? Is there a bed? Does it vibrate?"

Jennifer, on the other hand, got on the phone and spent several hours talking to strangers about their plumbing. We aren't renting a cabin, we're renting a bathroom with a rollaway cot.

"I need a bathroom I can use," she insists. (Technically, she needs two bathrooms and a portable make-up kit, but that's another column.) "And I have to make sure we aren't stuck in the boonies."

Call me naive, but isn't that the point of going to the mountains? It's supposed to be rustic, isolated, the kind of place a man can scratch himself like a Major League third baseman without worrying about offending the neighbors. My wife, however, wants a rustic and isolated cabin that is still within walking distance of a major shopping center: Mount Macy's.

I should mention that when Jennifer says "the mountains," she means the area around Boone, North Carolina, the outlet shopping capital of the world. So when she says "shopping," she means standing in front of an overflowing bin of irregular cut underwear at "Cooter's Country Barn Outlet" in Bohunk, NC. So when she says "vacation," she means "Michael gets to follow me around carrying shopping bags and whining about being hungry."

That's where I am right now. As you read this, I am in Rednecksburg, standing outside some store with a huge, ceramic Santa out front, going "Honey, let's skip this one, please!" Or I am in some cutsey "Kuntry Kitchen" buffet restaurant with farming implements hanging from the ceiling, ordering the "Dan'l Boone Buckwheat Hotcakes" and reading the *Wanker's Mountain Weekly*. Or I am standing in line for tickets to "Cleo and His Clogging Cousins: America's Only Clogging Elvis Review!"

As is so often the case on trips like these, I will end up having a good time. But it will be despite, not because of the trip itself. Sometime during the week, the breezes will be soft, the mountain air sweet and my wife and I will linger in a shady spot. And I will be happy.

Who knows, there may even be an unexpected eclipse...

July, 1995

HAVE YOURSELF A GENDER-NEUTRAL CHRISTMAS

Christmas used to be fun, didn't it? Remember all the presents and the parties, all the times we used to drink eggnog and go on sleigh rides and have our portraits painted by that nice Mr. Rockwell? Doesn't anyone remember that?

Me neither.

What I remember about Christmas is the fun of being a kid who is about to be buried under an avalanche of crass commercialism. Yes, for children Christmas is about stuff, loot, boodle. On December 25, our cry was "Presents! And keep 'em coming!"

Yeah, I know it's really about the baby Jesus and love and family and all that stuff, but the true vision of Christmas lives in the dazed, early morning eyes of children suddenly overcome by the true potential of a market economy. We watch with unadulterated joy as children are overcome by an overdose of sheer delight, each package affecting the child in the same manner that catnip affects a cat. We watch, and we vicariously share their delight.

That is why Christmas is indeed in the giving. Or used to be.

There was a time when, as a gift-giver, you were guaranteed at least a mumbled "Thank you" or insincere "Just what I needed!," no matter how lame the gift. A box full of Chia pets or a stack of Richard Petty commemorative hankies could get you through a holiday crunch, because you knew the gift-givees had all been taught to politely accept anything given at Christmas.

I learned this as a tot, when my family lived in Los Angeles. One Christmas, a progressive, Left Coast aunt gave me a doll--a stuffed, pale, rather effeminate-looking boy doll--a gift I ranked on the "Appropriate for an Impressionable Young Lad" scale somewhere between a pair of tights and tickets to *La Cage aux Folles*. Displaying my precocious sense of humor, I made some witty, endearing 6-year-old's remark ("Oooh, yuck! I think I'm gonna barf!") and found myself hanging by an ear in the nearest restroom while my mother applied a lesson in holiday etiquette on the lower end of my learning curve.

I learned to appreciate that doll on the ride home (extra padding), and I also learned we should be grateful for any gift we receive, no matter how quickly it ends up having its arms ripped off and facing the G.I. Joe firing squad. This may not have done much for my Christmas spirit, but I have been extremely easy to buy for ever since.

But now I am an adult, and the rules have suddenly changed. Gift receivers are no longer at the mercy of givers. Today, those who dare give gifts without considering the socio-political climate risk rejection, embarrassment and possible legal action. The innocent gift of a Hickory Farms Smoked Sausage Log to a vegetarian co-worker may be met, not with thanks, but a threatening glare or a late night "fund raising" call from PETA. Carelessly send Christmas cards featuring a Western European Santa and a non-culturally-diverse elfin work force, and you may wake Christmas morning to the sounds of Sister Souljah yowling "All I Want for Christmas is a Dead Honky" from beneath your tree.

This is particularly true when buying for children.

O.K., O.K., so Mommy doesn't want Junior to have a pop gun because he might grow up to vote Republican or support the Constitution, but can't the kid have any fun? How many gender-neutral ethnically-sensitive all-natural rain-forest-product toys are there? And who wants them? You can imagine how little River, Aurora or Pine Cone's eyes will light up when they get "The Children's Companion to Kafka: A Pop-Up Book!" Quick, kids: Find the cockroach!

Forget toy soldiers or squirt guns. Don't even think about knights in shining armor or dragons to slay (We don't slay our "Oversized Reptilian Companions" now do we, little Wheat Germ?)

And remember the Christmas fiasco of the Talking Barbie? Once the perfect Christmas gift for the pre-teen female on your shopping list, Barbie was beautiful, buxom, blonde and silent: the model of the ideal woman. (Just kidding!) Now, Mattel has given her voice, and while most of Talking Barb's comments are about parties, hair care and Ken (with one or two unkind remarks about Malibu Barbie's weight, so I'm told), her recorded repertoire included the comment: "Math class is hard!"

From the reaction, you would think little Barbie had called Hillary Clinton a Pro-Lifer. Across the political spectrum, from the far Left to the Very Far Left, women denounced Mattel Toys and their insidious plot to keep female math test scores from rising. "If we took half of the time we spend now reinforcing negative female stereotypes," they said, "and spent a third of it building positive role models, and one-eighth of it developing women leaders... no wait: O.K., you take a third of our women leaders, divide by two, then multiply the I.Q. we would have had if we been wasting time with the Easy-Bake Oven, no...."

The point is, if you give a child a Barbie she may love it, but her mom will whack you with her Gloria Steinem Cook Book.

So what is the only thing an adult can give school-aged children and be sure not to offend any politically-correct parents?

Condoms.

Norman Rockwell, where are you?

December, 1993

Chapter 4

RADIO GA GA

TELEVISION THAT PREACHES
AND CONSPIRES

"SCETV, where mendicancy demands a certain skittish caution..."--The State.

There is nothing more nauseating than watching a bureaucrat grovel to keep his job. The squishing of the soft spine as it genuflects, the slurping of lip against buttock, the pathetic whimpering as incompetent boot-lickers crawl from under their patronaged rocks, whining and pleading for one more snoutful from the public trough.

Yuck.

You can currently catch a glimpse of this repulsive process at SCETV (Educational Television) and SCERN (Spineless Cowards Employed Right Now!) where the "Not Employable in the Private Sector" Players ponder their career tracks in a future without federal funds. Kathy Gardner-Jones, the official "model-spokesperson" for SCETV wrote a blubbering editorial defending tax-funded TV because it gives South Carolinians "a choice."

Those zany kids at Public Television! Pro-choice on everything, except whether or not you have to pay their salaries.

The bureaucrats of PBS are in trouble, they say, because Radical Right Republicans led by the child-hating Nazi, Newt Gingrich, have twisted the results of the 1994 elections in such a manner as to insinuate that the GOP somehow "won." Now these radicals are claiming that Americans want "change," change that, in the warped minds of these Republican Neanderthals, involves "less government spending."

The horrifying result: Americans could face a future of Saturday nights...WITHOUT LAWRENCE WELK!

It's too hideous to imagine.

The issue of Government Television is actually bigger than "Can South Carolina survive without regular broadcasts of "This Old House?" The core question is, "What the heck is the government doing in the broadcasting business in the first place?"

In the past, there may have been a need for a taxpayer-funded network to reach small, rural markets where the only entertainment was AM radio and an occasional UFO sighting. Today the entire nation is served by commercial TV, 65 percent of America has access to cable, a digital satellite dish costs about 800 bucks, and you can rent *La Boheme* from your local video store for 99 cents.

Public TV? Why not keep the Pony Express, too?

And let's kill the disingenuous phrase "Public Television." *All* TV is public. Turn on your set and there it is. What PBS supports is "Government TV," a broadcasting network whose employees and programming are all chosen by the state. It's the US Postal Service with a video camera.

Every TV show is publicly funded. The difference is that commercial TV shows are funded by people who freely choose to sit down and watch them, while Government TV is funded by you, whether you watch it or not.

And chances are, you don't.

PBS's ratings have always been minuscule, and in prime time they usually rate somewhere between The Weather Channel and *Yan Cooks Cats* on Discovery. In the last five years, ratings have dropped an *additional* 20 percent, and government TV hacks have been struggling to recover viewers lost to commercial channels such as A&E and Nickelodeon.

Think about what that last sentence really means. First, it means that the marketplace works. If there are, in fact, people who want to watch four hours of British mumbling on *Masterpiece Theater*, the marketplace will respond--for FREE! In a few years, we'll have the All Opera Channel, the All Mozart Channel and even the "All Shows too Controversial to be Shown on SCETV" Channel, featuring any program about homosexuals who actually have sex, as well as a previously-censored episode of *Barney and Friends* in which Barney and Baby Bop do a little too much hugging.

Second, PBS s efforts to "recover viewers lost" to commercial TV involves convincing happy consumers to stop watching A&E and turn to a taxpayer-funded government service! Think about it this way:

Imagine you own a restaurant, one where you pay taxes and rent and try to make a living. The government decides it can't trust you to serve "good" meals, so it opens a restaurant across the street. Since it's a government establishment, it pays no taxes and, in fact, gets money from YOU, its competitor. Worse, when your restaurant begins to prosper, the government diner across the street announces it needs even MORE of your tax dollars so it can steal MORE of your customers!

The core premise of Government TV is indefensible and disgusting. The only intellectually honest reason for tax-funded "art" is the one you will never hear from Jane Seymour or the General Assembly: Elitism. America needs Government TV because you are too stupid to know what you ought to watch. And the less willing you are to watch it, the more important it becomes that you pay for it.

This is the Catch-22 of government. The more you refuse to watch *Boring, Old White Guys Talk Poetry* on PBS, the more likely it is to get your tax money; if it were a show you liked, you would watch it anyway and it would get high ratings and would make money on commercial TV so it wouldn't NEED your tax money. Thus, PBS, SCETV and other tax-funded arts endowments exist specifically to fund those works of art you would never fund yourself.

PBS's raison d'être is to offend, annoy or bore you. The minute it stops, it's A&E!

I write this, by the way, as a regular consumer of PBS and National Public Radio. I enjoy the programs and would miss them if they were gone. Then again, I enjoy the shows on HBO and Showtime, but I haven't figured out a way to get the government to pick up my cable bill every month. Defending my favorite programs on government TV is easy; it's just hard for me to defend making my neighbors pay the bill.

Oh, it can be done. You just need to develop a taste for well-licked boots.

January, 1995

SHUT UP!

Patriots, arise! Our Republic is in danger once again!

Terrorists? Floods in the Midwest? An Atlanta Braves pitcher on the mound in an All-Star Game?

Well, it's not *that* bad.

It's Talk Radio and, if you've read the papers, you know that radio talk shows are fraying the fabric of our free society, undermining the underpinnings of understanding, and serving red wine with fish at the dinner table of democracy.

Talk radio, in particular Rush Limbaugh, has come to represent, in the eyes of the left, everything that is wrong with America. It's so conservative. It's so disrespectful. It's so, well, *white*.

There are, of course, a plethora of urban talk shows targeting minorities, but let's not confuse the issue by interjecting facts at this late date. As I write, Congresspeople decry the "vocal minority" that insists on getting on the radio and talking about what Congress is actually doing. *Newsweek* magazine warns of "hate speech" from radio radicals who suggest that individuals are responsible for their own actions. And newspaper columnists bemoan talk show callers who cynically question the character of the president without clearing it with an editor first.

The essential complaint against radio talk is that the people who call are not "average," and therefore, not normal. National media outlets gave major play to a recent Times/Mirror poll showing that talk radio callers tend to be distrustful of government (in media lingo, "conservative"), have strongly held opinions they are willing to defend ("intolerant"), believe in individual responsibility ("cynical") and regularly attend church ("right-wing fundamentalist wackos"). It is only a matter of time before someone files a class-action suit against talk radio for civil rights violations. Soon these shows will only be available over the "Aryan Nations Network" or in the waiting area of your local Denny's.

As petty as the complaints about AM talk audiences are (one Public Radio pundit called Rush listeners "zombies"), there is truth in the core complaint: The audience does not represent the "average" American.

First, people who choose to listen to talk radio are, by definition, choosing NOT to listen to other radio programming, such as rock, rap or country music. By declining to sing along with Hank Williams Jr.'s "I'm Fat, Drunk, Racist and Proud!," talk radio fans immediately alienate themselves from the majority of their neighbors.

Second, talk stations have a lot of news. Listeners are assumed to have an interest in this news, and callers are expected to understand complicated phrases such as "trade deficit," "Gross National Product" and "Please turn down your radio!" Thus, compared to their FM counterparts, these people are Einsteins. In a society where college grads think "General Grant" was Lou's title before leaving the Army to become Mary's boss, talk radio callers can actually name members of their state legislature...including a few who *haven't* been indicted.

I agree with talk radio's critics that people who care enough about civic life (government, ethics, reason) to spend their leisure time talking about it do not represent the population at large. But this criticism applies to our entire democratic system. After all, it is extremely rare for more than 50 percent of eligible voters to turn out on election day, which leaves the workings of democracy to a suspect "voting minority."

Indeed, all decisions made in our democracy are made by an oddball minority, that small group of embattled taxpayers who still naively think that citizens can make a difference. So if it is the case that talk radio threatens America because callers don't resemble the population at large (i.e., callers can form complete sentences), how much more is democracy endangered by that "fringe" minority of people who actually vote in state and local elections?

The only way to ensure true representation of the American majority is to keep these dangerously civic-minded kooks away from the polls. If you are some radio-talk-show-calling weirdo who understands NAFTA or has read the second Amendment, you should not be allowed to force your will on your innocently ignorant neighbors.

I propose, therefore, that we revoke the voter registration card of any caller to the Rush Limbaugh program. Furthermore, I demand testing at every voting booth, and anyone who successfully identifies his or her legislator or understands the capital gains tax should be immediately disqualified from voting. This is the only way to give America the leadership it deserves.

I agree with Mencken: "Democracy is the theory that the average man knows what he wants and deserves to get it--good and hard."

July, 1993

CULTURE BORES

It began as an extremely flattering phone call.

"Is this the writer, Mr. Graham (Ooh, *Mister* Graham)? Mr. Graham, I teach a writing course at the University, and I am familiar with your work (Hey, he reads my stuff!). I think you'd be the perfect person to speak to my students on writing and journalism (Well, if Hemingway can't make it...). Are you available?

Sure!...I mean, well, I guess I could fit you in between book signings at the Library of Congress.

"I teach a course on multiculturalism, about the need for positive portrayals of women and minorities in the media. I'm trying to teach my students to avoid the negative stereotypes of racism and sexism. I'm concerned, however, about presenting only one side of the issue. After reading your columns, I thought you might be a good person to present the opposing view."

Oh.

Yeah, well, I'll grab my white sheet and a swastika be right over.

Thus I found myself cast as the token "angry white guy" for a bunch of journalism students. I denounced the evils of that infamous disease, "multiculturalism," though I'm not certain I know what the word means anymore. I've seen it used to describe everything from a general longing for people of all races to hold hands and sing "Kumbaya," to a specific, radical epistemology claiming that Beethoven was actually a homosexual mulatto woman from the Hopi Indian tribe. For the sake of this discussion, I will focus on the particular form of the p.c. virus that has infected the mainstream media.

Media multiculturalism might best be described as "looking for the *right* truth." That is, media outlets are actively pursing news stories that portray the world in the "right" way: white welfare recipients and black professionals; male nurses and female construction workers. When accurate reporting turns up the "wrong" story, it is set aside if possible, or written as "correctly" as possible...so that (true story) it is not uncommon for two crime stories to appear on the same page of the paper, the race of the white suspect prominently featured and the race of the black suspect unmentioned in the coverage.

The issue is not the race of the suspects in these stories, but rather the editorial decision that one robber's race was news and another's wasn't. This is why multiculturalism is bad for the media. It inevitably requires newspapers to violate Graham's Three Principles of Journalism:

On the newspage, always tell me what you really think happened: Despite what some readers think, they are just "news" papers, not "truth" papers. Mistakes will be made. But a newspaper should never get a story wrong on purpose. Trying to actively avoid offending minorities lends itself to deceit, as when Columbia, South Carolina's daily paper chose to intentionally misreport the cause of death in an "embarrassing" AIDS case. (For p.c. media-types, "embarrassing AIDS cases" are those in which the victim is NOT a happily-married working mom who teaches Sunday school.) Journalists are in the business of "who, what, when...." Multiculturalism stops at the "who," and then crafts the story to avoid negative stereotypes, especially in those cases when the stereotype happens to come true.

On the editorial page, always tell me what you really think about what you really think happened: In 1994, my hometown newspaper did something unimaginable in a world without multiculturalism: It published an apology for an *editorial.* Not a correction or clarification, but an apology for expressing an opinion on the OPINION page. Imagine a sports page apologizing because the wrong team won a game, or a business section lead that read "We're sorry this page is full of boring stock market stats, but...." Inconceivable.

Now, I have no doubt the opinion that inspired the apology was offensive. Hell, every opinion worth reading is offensive to someone. But we cannot have a serious dialogue on ideas if people are forced, by an adherence to multiculturalism, to apologize for opinions, or for offending people by the way they express those opinions.

Finally, a newspaper should never be afraid of words or pictures. For me, the low point of multiculturalism in the print medium was a recent front page story on a fractious NAACP meeting quoting one member calling another a "nigger" but spelled "n-----"

What a pile of c---. Either a person's statement is news or it's not. If so, print what they said. If not, cover something else. But don't treat me like a child, spelling words and whispering the naughty parts behind my back. I don't use the "N" word and I point out to people who use it around me that I find it offensive. But if the word is the news, use the word.

And don't avoid unflattering photos, either. If the truest snapshot of a newsworthy event is of an Italian guy named Vinnie with his shirt unbuttoned to his navel, eating a calzone and grabbing his crotch, forget trying to avoid stereotypes and run the photo. And don't run pointless photos of people doing pointless things just because the people in the photo happen to be minorities. It's condescending to them and confusing to me. Foolishly, I think there is some news related to these photos, just because they're published by a *news*paper.

Sheesh, you media people barely have enough time and newsprint to cover the REAL news. Leave the social engineering to B.F. Skinner.

April, 1995

THE BUTTHEAD MADE ME DO IT

In the America of the late 20th century, nothing is your fault. Nothing.

Weigh 900 lbs? It's not your fault. You're just calorically-challenged...here, have another bag of pork rinds.

Bust open some truck driver's head with a brick on national television? Hey, you're a victim of an unjust, oppressive society. And just think of your poor neighbors who can't even afford a brick! They deserve a cinder block subsidy. Let's just sing a few rounds of "Kumbaya" and all is forgiven.

Are you a college kid who spent a few late night hours lying in the middle of a busy roadway, only to discover to your amazement that you'd been run over by a Mack truck? "Disney made me do it! James Cahn is a bad role model--I'll sue!"

Burn down your house playing with matches?--"Mom, it wasn't me--it was Butthead!"

Little has changed since my youth when I tried blaming everything bad I did on Butthead, too (a.k.a., "my little sister"). But I never had the support of any major media outlets, and certainly not from the United States Senate where Buttheads have, historically, been well received.

If you aren't familiar with the "house burning" controversy surrounding MTV's Beavis and Butthead...well, don't ask US Senator Ernest F. "Incoherent Rambling" Hollings (D-Alzheimer's). Senator Hollings recently spent an afternoon on the floor of the US Senate (before someone finally helped him to his feet) railing against the socially-destructive MTV cartoon *Beavis and Barney*.

"I love you, you love me, let's microwave the neighbor's kitty!"

Or maybe was it *Beaver and Butthead*? (gee, Wally, let's torch Eddie's house--he's a geek!") I can't make out much of anything that is covered in Sen. Hollings' thick Charleston accent, but I do understand what he's getting at in his recent hyperventilations: freedom. There's way too much of it, and something must be done.

I will confess I have never watched a single minute of Beavis or Butthead, but it's my understanding that it is a crudely produced cartoon full of sophomoric humor, fart jokes and mindless destruction--so I assume it's making millions("No one ever went broke underestimating the intelligence of the American public"--H.L. Mencken). I will also confess I haven't seen *The Program*, the movie that inspired some drunk college kids to lie down on a busy city street.

But it doesn't matter, because the argument being made by the Neo-puritans such as Hollings and Janet "Fireball" Reno ("So, how many people have YOU set ablaze this week, eh Beavis?") is patently ludicrous. The pro-censorship forces argue that people who watch bad things being done in movies and on TV (setting fires, playing in traffic, hideous acting) will do those things themselves. Therefore, entertainment programs where these bad things happen (Beavis, *The Program*, any film with Jim Carrey) should be censored. In other words, it's "Idiot See, Idiot Do."

Don't talk to me about kids--they aren't the issue. Young children need some level of protection. The question is "from whom?" For example, when a supposedly "cartoon-inspired" house fire is set by a five-year-old, I have to wonder who is the biggest Butthead--the pyromaniacal cartoon character, or the parent who lets a preschooler play with matches?

And by the way: Has anyone else noticed that TV and movies only have the power to make people act more stupidly, never more intelligently? There were no complaints about bands of over-heated youths spouting poetry after *Dead Poets Society*, no concern that we would be overrun by streetwise algebra wizards when *Stand and Deliver* hit the box office. The problem isn't in the art--it's in the audience.

The issue is not danger to children; it's danger *from* morons. The error at the core of the pro-censorship argument is that we should protect stupid people from themselves by taking liberty away from everyone else. Stupid people shouldn't be allowed to have guns, so we'll make guns illegal for everyone; stupid people can't comprehend the concept of "fiction," so it's censored TV for all; stupid people shouldn't be allowed to vote--but Clinton's already president and we're just gonna have to live with it.

I'm waiting for a brave Senator to stand before the American people and denounce stupidity. I m looking for a true statesman who will say: "We don't need more government control of your lives, we need fewer idiots who are out of control! If you watch this crap, you're an idiot!" Will an American member of Congress ever deliver that message?

"What do you think we are--Buttheads?"

Heh, heh, heh.

November, 1993

71

MOTIVATIONAL SPEAKING

I was leafing through the local fishwrap not long ago, and I ran across several news stories regarding Republican presidential candidates, stories with similar, sinister spins:

"Republican presidential contender Phil Gramm of Texas, *courting the conservative wing of his party*, has threatened to tie the [Surgeon General] nomination up in a filibuster."

And "Senator Dole, *playing to the GOP right wing*, announced his support of the Tenth Amendment...."

This style of reportage is so common you may not even hear the cynical implications. If you believe what is written, Sen. Gramm's opposition to Dr. Foster isn't a result of personal conviction; it's political opportunism, a ploy to clear the church pews on election day. Sen. Dole is also acting on pure political motivation, pretending to be an advocate of the Constitution of the United States, when we all know he's a radical subversive.

This media myopia on motive is bipartisan: President Clinton's call for an increased minimum wage was labeled "shrewd" by *Time* magazine. "Minimum wage hikes appeal to the liberal constituency within the Democratic Party and working-class Americans," *Time* reported.

Now, I'm no high-falutin' journalist-type like Connie Chung or Geraldo Rivera, but isn't it just possible that President Clinton supports a minimum wage hike because he actually thinks it's a *good idea*? Could it be that Bob Dole really believes constitutional democracy is the way to go? And--here's a reach--isn't it at least possible that Phil Gramm spouts right-wing rhetoric because (this may sound shocking) he's a right-winger?

The issue of media coverage of motives was brought to mind recently by a friend who just graduated from USC's J-School. Diploma in hand and ready to strike out into the world of mass communications, she took time out to lecture me on ethics and public service. Her thesis: all politicians are essentially unethical. Why? Because part of their motivation, even when doing good, is self-interest. They hope their good deeds will get them votes. Because their motives are impure, everything politicians do is bad.

Her comments struck a resonant chord, because I have heard similar sentiments from so many press people. A newspaper editorialist recently told me he had never met anyone who acted in his own self-interest until he was in his twenties. Then one of his friends confessed to voting for Reagan hoping his own taxes would be cut. My friend the editorialist was shocked: "I couldn't believe someone would cast a vote just to help themselves."

I can't believe they let someone this naive near a word processor. I assume the Tooth Fairy tucks his columns under his pillow at night.

What results is what I call the cynicism of idealists, the notion that one selfish motive destroys all good actions. Thus, when Representative Jones stands up and offers a good idea--education reform, tax cuts, the mandatory sterilization of attorneys, whatever-- the only question the media has is "What's in it for Jones?" The political motive is the exclusive motive. If Jones' idea happens to be popular, he's even more suspect. "Giving the people what they want again, eh, Jones? You must be up to something..."

Don't get me wrong. Chances are, Jones IS up to something. Any grown-up capable of getting a job is smart enough to seize opportunities when they arise. But if every news story calls every popular action by every public servant a "political ploy," what's the point in reading the paper? You know the story before it's written.

Media people should be sophisticated enough to understand that almost every action involves mixed motivations. Why, for example, do churchgoers put money in the offering plate Sunday morning? Is it to obey God's command, or to avoid a cold glare from the usher passing the hat? And when you toss a dollar into the Jerry Lewis Telethon jar at the Get-N-Go, is it from pure generosity of heart, or the twinge of guilt that comes from wholeness of limb?

Or is it, as it is for most of us mortals, a little of both?

What I need to hear from the media when a candidate gives a fire-breathing speech before the NRA isn't the obvious story, "politicians-want-votes," but rather whether the speaker's record regarding gun control has earned him the nickname "Bazooka Bob" or "Pacifist Pete."

We all know tax cuts are popular with voters. What I want to know is whether Senator Blowhard's push for the flat tax began 20 years ago with a sudden rise in his tax bill, or 20 minutes ago with a sudden drop in his poll numbers.

This is a tough request to make of journalists, I know. It may require them to acknowledge that public figures sometimes mean what they say. It also takes reporters out of the easy arena of "He Said, She Said" journalism and into the less malleable realm of facts, records and actions.

Smart journalists are the first to admit that "getting the story perfect" is almost impossible. It's hard enough just to get the quotes right and make sure the names are spelled correctly. So why do reporters give so much coverage to the speculative realm of politician's psychology?

Perhaps they have ulterior motives.

May, 1995

RADIO GA GA

From the mailbag:

"Dear cretinous, right-wing scum: I am writing in regards to your Neanderthalish natterings about Public Broadcasting. What Rush-infested fever swamp did YOU crawl out of? If you would turn off the World Wrestling Federation for a few minutes and tune in NPR or McNeil-Lehrer, you might be able to understand why the few pennies of your tax bill used for PBS is the best money you've ever spent, even if you're too stupid to appreciate it.

Yours Truly, Barney.

Say what you will about the fans of PBS, but they are certainly literate...as evidenced by the high volume of hate mail responding to my recent column ("Television That Preaches and Conspires"). The correspondents' extensive vocabulary had me reaching frequently for my thesaurus just to keep up. When someone writes that you are a "nescient know-nothing, trapped in the dominion of absurdity," you know you've been dissed!

I am wrong about public television, they write, because I:
a) don't watch *Masterpiece Theater* or *NatureScene*.
b) watch too much *Hogan's Heroes* and *Gilligan's Island*.
c) can't tell the difference.

Government-funded and programmed TV and radio (liberals use the euphemism "public broadcasting") is good, they maintain, because:
a) They like the shows.
b) I have to pay for their favorite shows whether I like them or not.
c) Ha, ha.

In the weeks following my first criticisms of government broadcasting, I have been cornered at cocktail parties and caucus meetings by readers who absolutely insist that NPR and PBS are essential to the survival of our civilization. Why? Because the state is the sole source of "quality." To quote actual comments from actual liberals:

"Don't you like the shows? I mean, who else is going to do *Frontline* and *Sesame Street*?"

"I thought you conservatives were into values? [Government TV] is the only programming with values."

"TAKE AWAY MY SON'S BARNEY, AND I'LL KILL YOU!"

In short, the position of PBS defenders on the issue of budget cuts is the same hypocritical harangue heard from tobacco farmers, defense industrialists and other special interests who feed at the public trough: Don't cut MY pork!

Well, it's my pork, too. I am a regular listener of *All Things Considered* and a frequent viewer of *Washington Week in Review*. But in the age of multi-media, when Americans are adrift in an unmanageable tide of information from books, magazines, faxes, radio, TV, cable, satellites, online services, CD-ROMS--when there is, in fact, too much media--it is bizarre and embarrassing that the government would own its own media outlet. Even more bizarre is listening to liberals defend it based on the premise that we need the state to tell us what we "ought to" watch and hear.

I know you leftists are dazed and confused since the Gingrich revolution, so just a reminder: You guys are the ones *for* free speech and *against* government speech, remember? You oppose state control of media content, you're supposed to fear propaganda machines, even when they broadcast your propaganda. Is any of this ringing a bell?

The problem with government TV isn't the content; it's the concept. When you overwrought PBS defenders argue that we need government picking programs for us to watch because it picks "good" programs, you are setting yourselves up for the day when conservatives take over the PBS apparatus and hire their own program director. Are you willing to defend your precious public station when it begins broadcasting "The B-1 Bob Dornan Show" and "Homos Alone: Keeping Them in the Closet Where They Belong"?

If you really want to see government TV's full potential, spend a day channel surfing in Cuba or Iraq. Meanwhile, I am prepared to put my money where my mouth is.

So irrational, so nonsensical, so mind-numbingly absurd is the premise of government broadcasting in the digital age that I am making a challenge here and now. If one reader can offer me a single reasonable, legitimate and internally-valid argument for government radio and TV, I will treat you to a steak dinner at my favorite restaurant.

The glove has been tossed. Is there a Robert Byrd among you? Have any of you the spirit of Barney Frank or Ted Kennedy? Step up and make your case.

Big Bird is counting on you.

February, 1995

IT'S A WONDERFUL LIE

Of all the gluttonies indulged during the holidays, none is more vigorously enjoyed than the gluttony of ritual. The same old stockings are hung with care. The same old fruitcake is dragged from the attic, dusted off and set on the table. Mom's old Christmas albums, (the ones gas stations used to give away featuring has-been stars of the '50s) give the old turntable its annual workout. Then, with Andy Williams or the Andrews Sisters crooning in the background, the family gathers for the annual viewing of *It's A Wonderful Life*.

Thanks to the advent of cable TV, we Disco Babies (people who graduated high school after 1980) have had the story of George Bailey, Clarence the Angel and Mr. Potter etched on our collective consciousness. Before Ted Turner, few people had seen *It's a Wonderful Life* more than once or twice; today it is omnipresent. Cable TV features the "Wonderful Life Network" the week or so before Christmas, and rumors fly about remakes tentatively planned by MTV (*Bailey and Butthead's Excellent Adventure*), Black Entertainment Network (*It's A Wonderful Life--If You're a Rich Honky!*)and the 700 Club (*It's A Wonderful After-Life!*).

It certainly isn't a cheerful movie. I know, I know, you think the movie tells the heart-warming story of George Bailey, a man who in a time of crisis forgets all he has to be thankful for. Then, with the help of his guardian angel, Clarence, George sees the light one fateful Christmas Eve. That's the movie you *think* you've seen.

Well, think again.

Even the most hopeless optimist must admit George Bailey's life in Bedford Falls doesn't give him a whole heck of a lot to cheer about. First, he loses an ear drum when his show-boating brother falls through thin ice and George has to drag him out. Then he gets whacked 'til his ear bleeds by a drunk chemist who confuses "Hemlock" for "Hemorrhoid Medicine"--and this is all before George even makes it to high school. His career in pharmaceuticals over, George then slaves away in his dad's business, the Bailey Building and Loan, waiting for his younger, non-hearing-impaired brother to finish high school and enter the family sweat shop so George can leave Bedford Falls behind. Only, on brother's graduation night, Dad kicks the bucket and George gets roped into a job he hates while brother runs off to college, marries a beautiful girl, gets a cushy job with his father-in-law, and leaves George holding the bag.

Stuck in Bedford Falls, whose nightlife peaks at high school sock hops and cowtipping, George is easy pickings for the manipulating Donna Reed. Reed, a.k.a. "Mary," has had her eye on young George ever since she found out her classmate, Violet, had the hots for him. Mary snatches up poor George and pack up for their honeymoon...just in time for the Great Depression!

Their finances ruined, the Baileys move into a home that resembles Hitchcock's Bates Motel, but without the coziness. Life goes on, kids are born and given bizarre names (Zu-Zu?), and the Building and Loan stumbles forward--despite the incompetent book keeping of Uncle Billy, an Alzheimer's-afflicted family member who dabbles in bestiality. Said Uncle unwittingly drops an $8,000 deposit into the evil Mr. Potter's lap, and guess who happens to show up that day but the bank examiner, and as usual George is broke and well, that's when the movie really falls down.

For, despite having suffered the trials of Job, George Bailey is assigned a guardian angel straight out of Bureaucracy Hell. The Angel Clarence is an incompetent, low-level lackey in the Heavenly civil service, the type of no-brain government flunky who would have been fired immediately in the private sector but hangs on to his state job thanks to iron-clad union contracts. When Clarence appears, fresh from the customer service desk of the Pearly Gates Department of Highways and Public Safety, how does he help George with the problem of the missing money? Does he tell George where the money is, so the thieving Mr. Potter can be hauled into court and humiliated, clearly the most fair and self-evident solution?

Of course not! George is apparently missing the proper form, or stood in the wrong line or something, so Clarence makes him suffer even more by seeing the lousy life his family would have had if George hadn't been born.

This is the most confusing part of the film. The message is supposed to be "Your life is much richer than you think. Be grateful!" However, the glimpse of Bedford Falls without George is meaningless. Sure, everyone else is glad George is around--he's a sucker! What I want to see is George without Bedford Falls. Show me George on the beaches of St. Croix with the vixen Violet in one hand and a daiquiri in the other. Show me George's life as an employee of a real company that pays cash money, instead of the ever-insolvent Building and Loan. In short, show me George's life if he had lived it the way *he* wanted-- that's the Wonderful Life!

Instead, the so-called "happy" ending has George back home in the Dungeon, with the loud kids, the lousy job, and still $8 grand in the hole! His friends have to cough up their children's piggybank money while Potter keeps the cool cash. All this at Christmas, leaving George (and most of his neighbors, apparently) without a penny for presents. Clarence moves up in the Heavenly Highway Department, and George is stuck, once again, with the bag.

This is a wonderful life?

I've seen happier endings on Driver's Ed films.

December, 1993

Chapter 5

P.C.

Church Chat

Through no fault of my own, I recently found myself trapped in a Methodist church on a Sunday morning.

Nothing against churches on Sunday mornings, it's just that Methodist isn't my preferred flavor. Methodist, Episcopal, Unitarian; these soft-spoken, liberal, "Church of the Uplift" services leave me feeling like I've eaten too much salad: bloated but still hungry.

I like my religion with a little more red meat. I grew up in South Carolina's Pentecostal community, a thriving enterprise in the "I Found It" era of the late '70's. We called ourselves "charismatic" or "spirit-filled," but we were holy rollers just the same.

And roll we did. While snakes were never handled in my presence, in a rare, quiet moment of our Sunday evening prayer service the faint sounds of contented rattling could be heard nearby.

The Christians I grew up with were fervent and enthusiastic. We prayed loudly, desperately trying to drown out the sound of Satan, who often seemed to be clawing at our very door (it was usually just some neighborhood dogs drawn by the high-pitched howling). The reality of the spiritual world, below and above, pressed upon us. The outside world--the "real" world of politics, art and secular society--was rarely mentioned, except to point out that its destruction was nigh and weren't you glad, brother, just to be getting out in the nick of time?

The idea of a pastor preaching about "social justice" and "community awareness" was unimaginable. Our idea of social justice was when a local topless bar burned down early one Sunday morning.

I thought of my old Pentecostal friends as I slogged through this tepid Sunday morning Methodism. The preacher, or "ministerial companion" as he is sometimes known, despaired of the "shameful shortage of federal funding for our inner-city youth" with sincerity, if not actual passion. Not that Methodists and Unitarians don't get excited; just mention Operation Rescue or oppose socialized medicine, and fisticuffs could ensue.

More disappointing than the humdrum homily was the music. I've attended a lot of churches in my life and, no matter how uninspired the sermon or coma-like the congregation, I can usually find a moment of the sublime in the music. High church may mean low drama for us Pentecostals, but when it comes to music, nothing compares to the sacred hymns in the great Western tradition.

Or so I thought.

We turned in our hymnal to "Easter People Lift Your Voices" and my heart sank. The melody ("Angels From the Realms of Glory") is a classic of the 17th century, while the revised lyrics came from the 1970's. I suspect the BeeGees were involved.

First of all, what the heck is an "Easter Person" anyway? A few choruses later and we're singing "God has empowered us o'er our foes" *Empowered?* Why don't I go ahead and release my inner child while we're at it?

"Christ has brought us Heaven's choices" was another line that caught me off guard. I'm no theologian, but since when have there been any "choices" along the ol' straight and narrow way? And what do we choose from? First Class or Coach? Red, white or zinfandel?

The metaphor of Christ as maitre d' aside, the words "empower" and "choice" did not appear by accident. They are buzzwords of politically correct theology. A recent Wall Street Journal article revealed an invasion of mainstream churches by advocates of "inclusive" language; i.e. gender- and species-neutral names for The Big Guy (oops! make that "Big Person") in the Sky. Prayers have been written referring to God as "Father and Mother," "Grandfather, Great Spirit" and, my favorite, "Bakerwoman God" (They don't mean *that* Bakker woman, do they?).

My favorite hymns are subject to P.C. orthodoxy. A new hymnal praising the All-Powerful yet non-Ethno-Euro-Hetero-or Geo-Centric Being calls the Lord by the titles "strong Mother God," "Straight-talking Lover" and "Daredevil Gambler." While working the word "devil" into a proper noun describing the Most High is certainly clever, it is still somewhat disturbing.

Interestingly, the denominations working hardest toward this "inclusion" are the ones with the fewest members to include. Growth in the number of multi-racial congregations hasn't been in the mainline churches (two-thirds of a white Methodist congregation in Charlotte fled recently when a black minister was assigned to their church), but among the evangelical and charismatic faiths. In fact, attendance is falling among the Uplift congregations and growing among my folks back home.

Why? Because Americans like their religion hot and heavy. The want a Mighty God, A Terrible Swift Sword-Wielding God, the kind of God who openly excludes sinners, backsliders and IRS agents, and doesn't apologize for it. This is the kind of God who gets people excited, who gets your attention on Judgment Day, who can get you out of bed early on a Sunday morning.

People who believe in a familiar, limp-wristed and accessible God tend to sleep in on weekends. They like to listen to NPR, read the paper, maybe have a Bloody Mary. As the morning wears on, they may decide to just let this Sunday service slide on by....

If their God has a problem with it, what's She gonna do--bake some bread?

May, 1993

HOOTERS

In the great sea of stupidity, there is no bottom.

Case in point: Hooters Restaurant is being sued by a flock of well-plumed waitri who have secured legal counsel, claiming sexual harassment. If you've never been, Hooters is a wings-and-alehouse for the sort of juvenile gentlemen who think *Three's Company* was great television and consider the restaurant's slogan, "More Than A Mouthful," high comedy.

The walls are covered with posters of scantily-clad "Hooters Girls" doing bizarre pelvic stretches as they lie on the hood of a sports car. The waitresses at Hooters (there are no waiters) are aging teeny-boppers and unemployed aerobics instructors cashing in on their looks while the cashing is good. Stuffed into high-cut shorts and T-shirts still damp from the previous night's contest, these women sling wings and shake booty with energy and verve--all without mussing their hair.

This is not easy given the size of their coifs, usually the huge "mall hair" so popular among the gum-smacking types. Mall hair is poofy, but pulled back, flat everywhere on the head except for the huge part about an inch back from the forehead. This parallel part looks like a firebreak of exposed scalp and black roots, and beyond it is a stand of 40 or 50 stiff, towering bangs pointing forward from the head like an angry, hairy satellite dish. These women look as though, if you threw a pork chop over their heads, a long tongue would whip out, grab it and suck it back into their bodies.

Big hair. Large breasts. Tight clothes. Cheap beer. Hooters is the American Dream come true.

Or was, until a few ex-Hooter-ettes hired lawyers and started ruining the fun. According to the Associated Press, the plaintiffs claim they were sexually harassed at the workplace. They say the "atmosphere" at Hooters was oppressive, that customers felt free to make sexual comments about them, that male patrons ogled their anatomies and generally failed to show proper decorum in the presence of a lady.

At *Hooters?* It's hard to believe, I know.

Now, I am all for lynching an employer who demands sex as part of the job, or who forces his affections on his employees. But a waitress suing Hooters for promoting "an atmosphere that encourages sexual harassment" is like a GI suing the Army for promoting violence: Why did you think they were handing out all those guns?

Are Hooters Girls harassed? Of course they are. That's the point. Imagine a stripper down at the Pussycat Club stopping in mid-grind, looking at a patron and shouting: "Hey! What are YOU looking at?" Picture a prostitute dragging a client into court for making "nasty comments about my butt!"

What did these girls think? That Hooters was owned by radical environmentalists trying to save old-growth forests? The T&A atmosphere is self-evident, even to the sorority drop-outs working at Hooters today. If the bun-hugging uniforms weren't enough of a tip-off, how about the "Hooter Girls" calendars on the walls, or the name "Hooters" itself, a reference about as subtle as a mortician at a bungee jump?

I am in no way defending Hooters or the lowlifes who run the restaurants. When asked by reporters about the euphemistic name, the management unconvincingly pled ignorance: "You mean 'Hooters' means 'breasts?' We had no idea! We just liked the name...and besides, 'Yabos' and 'Bodacious Ta-Tas' were already taken."

A spokesman for the restaurant chain even told reporters: "Hooters Girls in our concept are put on pedestals (high enough to see up their skirts, no doubt)...We even put them on Hooters Girls trading cards." He would show them to you, but he would have to check I.D.s first.

The fact that there are Hooters, and women whose low self-esteem and/or IQs would permit them to work in them, is a sad commentary on our culture. But that fact in no way lessens the silliness of this lawsuit. I have no sympathy for either the morons who eat at Hooters or the cretins who run them. All I know is, you won't catch me wasting my lunch hour at that dump.

Not when they've got that great lunch buffet at the Pussycat Club...

October, 1993

85

VEG OUT

"You're not going to EAT that, are you?"

I froze, a forkful of filet inches from my mouth. My grad-student lunch companions stared me down, led by their disgusted young spokeswoman across the table. I glanced at my steak, at the plate, the floor, looking for the culinary danger they feared for me.

"Ugh," she moaned again. "You're eating meat."

Oh, no: veg heads!

From around the table came protests of proteinian piety, interspersed with denunciations of my flesh-eating, Eurocentric world view. It is my experience that there are two kinds of vegetarians--one group benign, the other malignant. This group was decidedly malignant, perhaps even fatal.

Benign vegetarians are those health food aficionados who eschew meat for dietary reasons. They fear that beef and chicken might expose them to things that violate their lifestyle, such as flavor and pleasure. These people are usually dead and buried before they turn 50, victims of their gross thinness in both body and spirit. When I encounter these sproutheads, I pass peaceably and try not to snicker too loudly.

Then there are the "Vegetarians of Virtue," people whose moral principles prevent them from eating meat...or from allowing nearby diners to enjoy their meat-and three-veg in peace. These veggers are filled with evangelical fire. They cannot let a public meal go by without pronouncing judgment on the congregation of comestibles: Fish--a close call; chicken--not for the true believer; beef--let the Lord rain fire from above!

And they love to argue, as I discovered at lunch. The first argument they hit me with was based on the premise that all animals are equal--a boy is a pig is a fish is a slug is an attorney (although the slugs aren't too happy about the last part). And man, as equal member of the animal kingdom has no "right" to go around killing fellow Earth beings. Killing an animal, ANY animal, is murder.

Unfortunately, this is a lousy argument for vegetarianism. First of all, animals die violently every day at the hands of their fellow "Earth beings." It's called the food chain. Fish eat worms, bears eat fish, and, eventually, worms eat us all. So, until one of these "Meat is Murder" kelp-eaters volunteers to step forward and slap the trout out of Smokey Bear's hand, these crimes will continue. Using this vegetarian "logic," the world is filled with murder every day, and Janet Reno should be shutting down *NatureScene* instead of *NYPD Blue*. The only moral universe for these vegetarians is one of "Beansprouts By Force," where every carnivore and omnivore is locked in a cage, and all decisions about health and diet are made exclusively by our moral superiors--in other words, it's the Hillary Health Care Plan.

By the way, that's what we humans are: omnivores. Therefore, what goes for our "moral equals"--bears and bald eagles--goes for us, unless you think our large intestine is there just for looks. The single most irrational argument made by vegetarians is the denial that humans are natural predators (a.k.a. "meat eaters"). Vegans: Wake up and smell the bile! We didn't evolve incisors just to rip open the cellophane on the tofu box.

Of course, as a human you can choose to eat only plants, but that doesn't make you an herbivore any more than choosing to live the rest of your life crawling on your hands and knees would make you a quadruped. But just because a lifestyle decision is possible doesn't make it reasonable. And mistaking the possible for the reasonable doesn't make you right: It only makes you annoying.

My leftist lunchmates moved on to vegetarian argument #2: "Of course it's not morally wrong for bears to kill their prey--it's only wrong for people, because we KNOW better. We can reason, we can moralize, we can figure out how to take soy beans and make high protein foods that taste like congealed leisure suits. We are a superior species, we govern the planet, if you will, and vegetarianism is good government."

This argument comes straight from the Pat Robertson play book. It's the old "stewards of the planet" theory, which sounds a lot like the even older "White Man's Burden" theory, which was used to justify colonialism and slavery. The idea is that one group is superior--in this case, people--and another group, animals, are inferior but morally equal. We must manage and care for them.

Once you accept that premise, the logical conclusion is that a pig is *not* a boy is not a cow, and the rest is easy: Fire up the grill! Why not? They're only animals. One theory of "proper management" (game preserves) is no better than another (Roast lamb with mint preserves). It's simply an argument among the responsible over the fate of the "inferiors."

Thus, "moral vegetarianism" is as sensible as "managed competition." Either every animal death in nature is a tragedy, in which case vegetarians should advocate a worldwide zoo system to put cheetahs and crocodiles on Kibbles-N-Bits; OR, humans are the only animals who can understand "death" as moral or immoral, making us the superior species upon which the rest can make no moral claim.

Once again, I have no problem with people who are in biological denial. I'm from the "That just leaves more Bar-B-Q for me" school of dietary science. What I do have a problem with is vegetarian self-righteousness. Nothing is more annoying than people who are very, very loud and very, very wrong at the same time. If you're going to make primary lifestyle decisions based on irrationality, that's your business. Just be smart enough not to brag about it. That's all I ask.

The problem, I concluded as my lunch companions as they meekly picked at their pasta salads, is that you vegheads haven't got your logical ducks in a row.

And them ducks is good eatin'.

November, 1993

HIGH SCHOOL CONFIDENTIAL

I was a teen-age sexual harasser.

Thanks to a publicity campaign launched a by a group of feminist academics (The National Institute for Angry Women Desperate to Hold a Press Conference), my secret shame, and the shame of America's junior high schools, is now revealed. After years of detailed research and expensive federal studies, we now know, beyond a shadow of a doubt, that America's 13-18 year-old population thinks about sex. Ah, the miracles of science....

According to a recent report, "Naughty in the Ninth Grade: How Reaganomics Turned Our Children into Perverts," the vast majority of public school students are exposed to (and I quote) "sexual jokes, comments, and looks." Some students are even "touched" and "pinched" in a sexual manner by classmates.

I realize this is hard to reconcile with our image of public schools: clean, quiet halls of academe, where polite, intellectually stimulated students spend their days discussing *King Lear* and Al Gore's book on global warming. However, I can testify from personal experience that this is simply not the case.

You see, as a student I was guilty of all the offenses above. I was a virtual classroom Clarence Thomas, the Bob Packwood of Pelion High.

Sexual jokes? If my classmates were enraptured by the poetry of Maya Angelou, I failed to notice. My friends and I were spinning rhymes about a certain young lass from Nantucket, who...well, let's just say it was not high art.

Sexual comments? My friend Scott Deans and I once had a contest to see if we could twist every classroom statement made by our teacher into a sexual innuendo. We made it successfully through five class periods and halfway through Algebra III before a particularly graphic comment about "inverted integers" got us sent to the principal's office.

As for sexual looks, I must confess that I'm not sure what a sexual look is. But I once pulled a muscle by repeatedly dropping and picking up the same pencil 47 times in one class period attempting to confirm unsubstantiated reports that Denise Elmwood was not wearing any underwear.

Yes, I was a victimizer, a user of impolitic language, insensitive to the harm done to others. When I referred to Sally Hall as "Sally Hall, Flat as a Wall," I wasn't "making fun" of her anti-Partonesque features: I was committing violence, reaffirming the male-dominated society's vision of feminine beauty.

But I was also a victim. How can I describe the shame and embarrassment when Russ Williamson and Kelly Collins sneaked up behind me and pulled down my gym shorts while I was distributing "sexual looks" from the sidelines of Junior Varsity Girl's basketball practice? That one moment cost me a lifetime of self-esteem, not to mention $24.75 the following week for an inflatable jock strap.

But I am not making excuses. I am prepared to apologize, to pay for the social costs of my actions, to perform penance (in a fit of remorse I recently purchased every Sinead O'Connor CD available in the US, though I have yet to feel guilty enough to actually listen to them). I simply did not realize that I was contributing to the demise of public education.

When feminist academics stepped forward to "break the silence" about teen-agers and their obsession with the "naughty bits," they described the actions I've confessed to as part of a "crisis" in our schools. "How can we expect our children to learn in this environment?" one Purita--I mean Professor--demanded.

She may have a point. I managed to escape from the South Carolina school system (Motto: "Where Literacy is Optional") with virtually no education whatsoever. However, trapped as I was in my Euro-Hetero-Gendero-centric World View, I naively assumed that my lousy public education was the result of using textbooks written during the Truman administration. I blamed my science teacher who thought "fission" was one of the primary industries of the Gulf coast states for my ignorance on matters scientific.

Silly me. What our schools need isn't higher standards or competent teachers: We need less hormonal oppression from culturally insensitive students who talk dirty during homeroom. The way to kick Germany's industrial butt (as opposed to "pinching" it, which is now strictly Verboten) isn't by demanding that students master the subjects of math and science--it's by insisting that they avoid the subjects of spin-the bottle and heavy petting.

So, as my final penance for my sins, I hereby volunteer to spend one day a week monitoring classrooms in our public schools. And the first student to pull a pigtail, pinch a passerby, I will personally throw out on his or her...ear.

Hey! You in the back--stop dropping that pencil!

June, 1993

BOOMERS

Try to imagine this scene: A crowd of adults gather at a city park to enjoy a performance by rap artists 2 Dead Doggs, who are serenading the throng with heart-warming ballads like "Yo! My Ho is a Bitch" and "Yo! My Bitch is a Ho."

Suddenly, a gang of high school drama students show up at a nearby parking lot and begin a rowdy recitation of scenes from *As You Like It* at the top of their voices. The echoing iambic pentameter drowns out the concert, interrupting a particularly poignant rap ballad on the non-traditional romantic aspects of a .45 slug in the groin. Worse, these theatre-crazed kids scandalize the rap patrons by emphasizing bawdy parts of Shakespeare's work, loudly interjecting the word "codpiece" in textually-inappropriate places.

Unable to hear the nuances of the moving lyric refrain "Kill the m-----f----- cops! Kill 'em dead!," a few of the rap-art lovers walk over and complain to the dramatists. Alas, the uncivil Shakespeareans ignore them. The rap concert is ruined, the evening is a disaster, and the ensuing controversy causes City Council to enact an ordinance restricting all performances of Elizabethan verse to daylight hours.

Of course, this is a joke. It is the mirror image of a scene played at a public park in Columbia, South Carolina recently when an audio bombardment of Snoop Doggy Dogg drove the anemic allies of the Bard of Avon from a "Shakespeare in the Park" event without a fight.

But why is this scenario dismissed as a joke? If you believe, as the executives of Time-Warner claim to, that the "art" of rap is a vital part of America's cultural life, then why shouldn't "Rap in the Park" supersede Shakespeare?

This is, after all, the core argument of multiculturalism. *As You Like It* only *seems* artistically superior to NWA's "F--- the Police" because of our mainstream cultural bias. George Sand and the Geto Boys are artistically equivalent, once you get past ethnocentric prejudices that cloud your ability to enjoy the sound of illiterate morons screaming obscenities for no apparent reason. So, how can the Limousine Liberals who dominate America's city councils support the cultural oppression of forcing art lovers gathered in public places to turn down their boom boxes?

Because, despite lip service to multiculturalism's political agenda, no thinking adult in America--Republican or Democrat--believes it for one second. No adult believes rap is "art," any more then they believe Bob Dole is actually offended by it. Rappers (I refuse to use the oxymoronic "rap artists") aren't musicians--they are bad poets with drum machines. In fact, rap is to music as masturbation is to sex: The former resembles the latter just enough to remind you what you're missing.

Taking rappers seriously is only slightly more ludicrous than taking rap listeners seriously. I know that young people can't be held responsible for their musical tastes (through an embarrassing set of circumstances, I left high school with a complete set of Queen albums). But that does not relieve adults of the burden of showing our disdain. We have a duty to let these misguided children know that rap will be for their generation what disco was to mine: a horrible, horrible memory. With lots of bad clothes to match.

Yet, few American intellectuals are willing to stand up and say "Shakespeare is good, Tupak Shakir is bad." Not morally bad, not culturally evil: just plain bad art. I'm not picking on rap: country music, Hollywood films, any book with Fabio on the cover--all are to be avoided when possible. But saying that one artist's work is "good," and another's is "bad" involves making judgments, the being judgmental is the last universally-agreed upon social sin.

Judging others also requires courage, a willingness to defend one's conclusions in public. And in contemporary America, courage is in extremely short supply.

Our failure--at the park, in the record store, at the stoplight next to the self-propelled, purple sound system with vanity plates--is a failure of resolve. Instead of standing up to clueless kids and saying "Hey! This is Shakespeare, show some respect," we send in the police to take away their boom boxes. Instead of fighting the real cultural war, we send in the jackboots--not because the music is lousy, merely because it's too loud.

One day, the kids are going to call our bluff. They'll start roaming public parks carrying boom boxes with Mozart cranking at fifty decibels. What happens then? The "Piano Concerto in D minor" (K.466) will join "Cop Killer" in the annals of American art.

June, 1995

WORKIN' FOR A LIVIN'

"The law is the law, no matter how ridiculous it might seem to some people."
--Ron Shigeta, Los Angeles' Disabled Access Division

Mr. Shigeta, the West Coast bureaucrat quoted above, deserves a special place in the hallowed halls of local government. He should be given the bureaucrat's Bronze Star, the Order of the Obsequious, and the Congressional Medal of Moronity. For, in a single action, he has revealed the true nature of government in America.

Mr. Shigeta is the bureaucrat who recently shut down "The Odd Ball Cabaret" in LA. The Odd Ball is a strip club ("titty bar" in the vernacular) whose featured attraction was a fully-operational shower on-stage. Women would give "demonstrations in personal hygiene" while local perverts ogled, drank overpriced beer and waited to grow a brain.

Enter Mr. Shigeta, the Americans with Disabilities Act (ADA) administrator in Los Angeles. His eagle eye detected that the stage show shower stall was NOT WHEELCHAIR ACCESSIBLE, thus denying handicapped women the right to publicly "soap up" for the Odd Ballers. These poor, disabled damsels were denied their constitutional right to "shake their showered booties." Who would speak out for the exhibitionists without extremities?

Ron Shigeta, that's who! He sprang into action and promptly shut down the Odd Ball Cabaret for violations of US Code 32 section 40-

13-9, subsection-J-12, 386 MHz with 4 meg RAM, "Operating a Successful Business Without the Government's Permission."

Hangin's too good for 'em.

Before the ADA, a job interview at a Los Angeles strip club might have gone like this: "So, baby, you want to be a stripper, eh? Let's see...are you willing to publicly prance about naked for money? Good...do you have incredibly low self-esteem? Good...and are you missing any major limbs or organs...Uh oh!"

Today, thanks to social justice ala Shigeta, America's quadriplegic cuties and exhibitionist amputees can revel in their right to take it all off...or could have, except the Odd Ball is now closed for business. As is so often the case, right-wing reactionary types who own businesses and pay the bills don't see the social value in adapting their workplaces to people who are inherently un-hirable. After all, think of what would happen if a wheelchair ridin' momma actually applied for a job at a strip joint?

We all know that the first club owner tasteless enough to open a handicapped dancers' strip club (Women, Whips and Wheelies--Live To-Nite!) would be denounced as a deviant and run out of town by the same liberal wackos who supported the ADA to begin with. So the point of the ADA isn't to get you to actually *hire* a handicapped person, no, no, no. You should just spend thousands of dollars so you *could* hire them, even though you'll be a social pariah if you do.

Fortunately, few people (outside the state of Arkansas) are willing to pay money to see naked amputees. It's also hard to believe the intent of Congress in passing the ADA was to break up the "Two Legger's Cartel" in the area of adult entertainment. But that doesn't stop a dedicated government employee like Ron Shigeta: "The law is the law, no matter how ridiculous it might seem to some people," he proclaimed--implying that, to Shigeta, the law seems perfectly reasonable.

The problem is that politicians, and the voters who elect these idiots, don't understand the pragmatic effects of their actions. No one wants to see qualified workers shut out of jobs because they're handicapped. But that doesn't mean we should give government the power to force businesses to "be good," with the word "good" interpreted by your local bureaucrat. Great ideas like protecting the handicapped inevitably end up with people like Ron Shigeta shutting down symphony orchestras for failing to hire deaf violinists. Despite all the "reinventing government" gibberish coming from President Clinton & Co., we all know how government really works. It's the government that requires drive-through bank ATM's to have Braille keypads; it's the government that forces gas stations to post "No Smoking" signs above each pump of explosive, flammable liquid; and it's the government that requires airplanes flying from Atlanta to Omaha to provide floating seat cushions in case the plane makes an emergency landing in the Pacific.

In short, it's the government's job to make us act even more stupidly than we would have if we had been left alone.

So today, I salute Ron Shigeta, and the thousands of Shigetas who are defending the common good at taxpayers' expense. If stupidity were a recognized handicap, your government would be the most progressive employer in the world.

May, 1994

FINISHED

"The theory [of college] is that a plow hand, taught the binomial theorem and forced to read Washington Irving, a crib to Caesar's "De Bello Gallico" and some obscure Ph.D's summary of <u>The Wealth of Nations</u>, with idiotic review questions, becomes the peer of Aristotle and Abraham Lincoln....It is, I fear, a false theory: he simply becomes a bad plow hand--perhaps with overtones, if Mendel is kind to him, of a good Rotarian."--H.L Mencken, June 6, 1927.

With summer upon us, I've been bumping into newly-issued intellectuals from the American university system at every social function. These young people are pleasant enough, usually appropriately dressed, and seldom use the wrong fork. Beyond these limited social skills, however, I am unwilling to speculate.

Spend five minutes with the typical "Graduation X"-er, and you will come to the ominous conclusion that someone, somewhere, has been screwed out of $50,000. Only larceny can explain how a mind can spend four years under educational siege but remain untouched by the experience.

This is the majority of our college grads: English Lit. majors to whom the name "Swift" is only an adjective; chemistry students who think Avogadro's number is part of a guacamole recipe. Yes, a handful students go to college intent upon learning, and others are occasionally proselytized into a voluntary education by an enthusiastic teacher or personal renaissance.

But the majority of college students in America have no more interest in a "liberal education" then a preacher's son has in Wednesday night Bible study. They suffer their classes as unavoidable interruptions between keggers and rounds of "Full Contact Sorority Diving," without the vaguest notion why anyone would care in the least about Western Civ. or Stats. They look upon their graduation as a draftee looks upon the end of a war. Finally, they sigh, it's over.

Why, then, do these people go to college, and how the heck do they graduate?

The answer to the first question is found in the steady drip of bourgeois bilge dispensed by high school guidance counselors. Every high school student who can sit up without drooling is urged to chase the American Dream at their local college campus. It's simple, they are told: Go to college. Get a good job. Be happy. This is a plan the most simple-minded sophomore can understand.

The colleges aren't run by dummies, either. Colleges aren't in the business of keeping students out, or flunking people who still have available credit with the Student Loan Administration. Even bad students can make good, paying customers. Thus, entrance standards have fallen so low some football players have stopped cheating on the SAT, and colleges courses are now graded on curves so extreme they make Dolly Parton blush.

Once again, there are exceptions. Students who plan careers in academics, medicine, and the like belong in universities. But it is unfair to force them into classes filled with vo-tech wannabes who dilute the value of expensive diplomas. So valueless have college degrees become, they no longer have any connection to adult life. What does it mean, for example, to have a degree in biology? That you are a biologist? Of course not! Most employers wouldn't let a B. S. "biologist" handle a urine sample without additional training. What about one of my personal favorites, a degree in "drama?" Does this make you an actor? I think not, Olivier. You learn to act by acting, not by taking courses on "Transgender Themes and Multicultural Motifs in the 'Ernest' Series: A Jim Varney Retrospective."

What a college degree means today is what a high school diploma meant a generation ago: You have met the minimum educational requirements for full social standing. It is a $50,000 prom ticket, your permission slip to roam the halls of adulthood.

It is also four years you didn't spend starting your own business. Four years you didn't write, didn't act, didn't paint. Four years you weren't learning how bridges are built by actually working on one.

A friend once told me she thought of college the way people used to think of finishing school. The difference, I replied, is that after college you haven't "finished" anything.

In fact, you're just starting.

June, 1995

THANK GOD FOR HITLER

I offer the following for your consideration:

--From a recent letter to the editor: "[Columbia, SC] Mayor Bob Coble and Sen. Darrell Jackson endorse Nazism and fascism! By publicly coming out against a referendum on the Confederate battle flag, these two 'public servants' are aligning themselves with the beliefs of Hitler and Mussolini....So here's to Bob and Darrell--Sieg Heil!"

--During a debate over budget cuts, Congressmen John Lewis of Atlanta infuriated Republicans when he said their plans to cut programs benefiting children, poor people and the disabled was "reminiscent of crimes committed in Nazi Germany."

--In Pompano Beach, FL, a lawyer was removed from court for wearing short pants, a violation of the judge's dress code for working attorneys. As she was led from the courtroom, an angry friend shouted at the judge: "You're the heel at the foot of the fascist boot!"

--The New Yorker Magazine reports that Vice President Al Gore, as a college student writing home to his father, once cited the US Army as an example of "fascist, totalitarian regimes."

Where would we be today without Hitler? Politically and rhetorically, old Uncle Adolph is America's best friend. It is virtually impossible to listen to an extended discussion on social or political issues without hearing echoes of the jackboot.

House Democrats accuse the Republican leadership of using "Nazi tactics" in pushing their legislative agenda. Rush Limbaugh calls radical feminists "Femi-Nazis." Libertarian commentator Samuel Francis calls anti-smoking activists the "Smoke Nazis."

Look to your Left, or look to your Right: There's a Nazi behind every treatise.

What is this rhetorical obsession with Adolf Hitler? Sure, he's a heinous example of the unfathomable depths of human evil, but human evil is hardly a novelty. The Japanese subway gassers, Colin Ferguson,

Susan Smith, Maury Povich--these are just 1995's candidates for Satan Incarnate.

When looking for examples of evil, why do we always reach for a Nazi? Why not, say, a Menendez? I think we'd all agree that these are monsters in human form, sick and disgusting individuals who committed heinous crimes...unfortunately, we don't "all" agree. That's the problem. There is at least one juror in California who believes that these poor boys are innocent victims, not vicious killers. Thanks to that juror, these two murderers remain unconvicted.

It's true the Menendez boys only killed their parents, while the Nazis tried to wipe out an entire race, so perhaps we use the "Hitler Standard" because he is evil's number one volume dealer. If that's the case, the name Stalin would be commonplace and Communism, not Fascism, would be the "ism" of choice for struggling debate squads. After all, more people have died at the hands of communists in my short lifetime than were killed by Nazi Germany.

Why isn't Stalin the standard-bearer for universal evil? Because America has a history of sympathy for Leftist goons. Throughout the Cold War, at the height of Soviet expansionism, many prominent Americans continued to urge detente with Soviet aggressors. Now, try to imagine an op-ed piece urging "cooperation" with the Nazis.

Compare this to the media's eye-rolling reaction when President Reagan used the phrase "evil empire." In the mainstream media, there is no American consensus that totalitarianism per se is wrong, only "Right-Wing" totalitarianism, which is why the Anti-Defamation League recently accused members of the Christian Coalition of having "Nazi sympathies," but had no problem holding its tongue through decades of Communist regimes around the world.

Apparently, Pat Robertson is more evil than Pol Pot.

In the end, the reason our society needs Hitler is because we need "easy-to-define" evil. In a nation where tolerance is perceived as the greatest good, calling someone "evil" smacks of judgmentalism. It could be argued that the only true evil in American society is judging someone else's actions as evil. So we are only prepared to condemn those examples of evil that are so extreme as to be beyond judgment, such as the evil of the inhuman Nazis.

Or the evil of people who are judgmental.

Short of the Third Reich, therefore, Americans are hesitant to condemn anything. The deadly riots that followed the first Rodney King verdict, for example, would seem indisputably "evil." Angry crowds gather in the street to protest a jury verdict (mob rule), they loot, beat and kill people--some because of the color of their skin (racism)--and they burn down whole neighborhoods (ethnic cleansing). If ever there were a contemporary incident of evil, this would seem to be it.

But on National Public Radio that very weekend, I heard a commentator complain that using the word "riot" to describe what happened in LA was "unfair." "What about the 'riot' of neglect," he asked." What about the 'riot' of poverty? What about the 'riot' of cuts in social spending?"

Yes, the riots of Reaganism. These thugs weren't maiming, killing and stealing--they were merely expressing opposition to the capital gains tax cut.

In a society that is unwilling to condemn blood-thirsty rioters, murdering Menendez's and the carnage of Communism, evil is almost impossible to name.

So, I say "Thank God for Hitler." At least someone is getting the credit he deserves.

March, 1995

Chapter 6

IN THE NEWS

O'Justice

The programming director for the "All O.J. Network" needs to beef up the nightly line-up. Things are getting so boring at the Trial of the Century that people are beginning to talk about the actual court case.

Uh-oh! Better fire up the blow dryer and send in Kato!

Things are so out-of-hand that some attorneys are talking about the case even though they aren't being paid for it! Admittedly, there are only a dozen or so lawyers left in America who haven't been hired by either the defense or a cable network to analyze the trial. But I happened to run into a couple of these left-out lawyers and here's what they had to say about the O.J. Simpson trial:

"Oh, it's terrible," clucked one. "A fiasco. Makes attorneys look like overbearing, self-promoting jerks."

"I know it," concurred his fellow litigator. "It's really putting our legal system in a bad light...and it's hurting my business, too."

"Really?" relied his friend. "Have you thought about suing? Class-action, maybe?"

"Hmm, there's a thought...."

Believe it or not, America's attorneys are on a tirade about the Simpson trial. They claim it is a perversion of the legal process, that the millions watching are losing their long-held faith in our justice system.

I'm not too worried about the typical O.J.-watchers and their view of American jurisprudence. These are the people who thought the Clarence Thomas hearings were held to find a replacement for Chief Justice Perry Mason. Instead, let's seriously consider the premise, held by many, that there is something "wrong" with the Simpson trial.

I couldn't disagree more.

The O.J. Simpson trial is, quite simply, the American justice system at its best. This is what our judicial machine looks like when it's humming on all eight cylinders. It features one of the best prosecutors in the nation and the best defense team money can buy. The judge is experienced and well-seasoned, and the jury was filtered through a textbook selection process.

Litigationally speaking, folks, it don't get no better 'n this!

Sure, we all know that O.J. is guilty as hell but has more chance of becoming Grand Goober of the KKK than he does of being convicted, but that's beside the point. The *system* is working great!

"What about justice?" you ask. What does justice have to do with the American court system? Ask any honest lawyer (oxymoron alert!) and he will tell you that whatever relationship you may see between what is just and what happens in a courtroom is purely coincidental. You see, in the American system, no one other than the jury is charged with the pursuit of justice.

Certainly not defense attorneys. The O.J. defense team has absolutely no interest in the accurate application of justice, given that their client spent the night of the murder Armor-All-ing the remains of the deceased off his dashboard. The defense attorney's job is not to pursue truth but rather to promote doubt. They must convince the jurors that the world is flat, that the sun sets in the East, that mysterious, knife-wielding extra-terrestrials wore one of O.J.'s socks.

The prosecution's duty is identical, only they are headed in the opposite direction. Their job is to get a conviction, period. Instead of seeking to present the jury with all available information, they are contesting clearly admissible evidence and attacking the credibility of competent witnesses such as South Carolina's Nobel Laureate, Kary Mullis. (Mullis, by the way, proves that, despite surfboards to the head, multiple hits of LSD and the lamest public school system in America, you can't beat a great set of genes.)

The prosecutors have no more vested interest in truth or justice than Johnny Cochran or F. Lee Bailey. They just happen to have a guilty defendant. If this were *The People v. Mother Theresa*, Marcia Clark would present evidence that rosary beads are lethal weapons.

That leaves only the judge to pursue the truth. However, his job isn't the truth, either. He's only there to make sure everyone plays by the rules...or cheats in the same way, whichever is easier. The Simpson trial is being overseen by the now-infamous Judge Ito, who is doing his best to stretch it out into the next presidential election. But the slow tempo caused by Judge Ito's media-driven paranoia is not hurting this case.

In fact, to denounce the O.J. show as a "bad" trial begs the question: "What is a good trial?" One with railroading judges, lame witnesses and questionable evidence? One where the defense attorneys are uninterested in the outcome? Where all the jurors are in a rush to get home and watch *Wheel of Fortune*?

It is true that the Simpson trial is not a typical court proceeding. O.J. is the only black man in America who could have stabbed a white woman to death and not have been plea-bargained into solitary by now. However, the Simpson trial does represent what every citizen, in theory, is supposed to get. The distance between this trial and "regular" American justice is what is destroying faith in our system.

In other words, the Simpson trial is "bad" precisely because it is so good. If you think you disagree, ask yourself one question: If you were accused of a crime and faced life in prison, would you want the typical courtroom performance, or the Simpson defense team on your side?

Case closed.

April, 1995

103

GOD'S GEEKS

As a graduate of Oral Roberts University (I have a degree in fund-raising) and a life-long student of the Christian faith, one of the lessons I have learned is this: No one is too stupid for Jesus.

There is an entire social class inhabiting the churches and seminaries of America, a group I call "Geeks for God." They are life-losers, social flotsam who have washed from rejection to rejection-- Rotary clubs, Amway meetings, bowling leagues--learning nothing and annoying everyone they meet. They eventually end up at a church social or neighborhood Bible study, and experience a Damascus Road revelation: "These people HAVE to like me, no matter how big a jerk I am--if they don't, they go to Hell!"

Having had one of these guys for a college roommate, I sincerely recommend the latter.

God's Geeks attend every single service, including the weddings of strangers (what else are they going to do?). They take copious notes during church services, notes that prevent them from having to understand what is being said. Their faith substitutes for an actual life, a crucifix conveniently filling in for the cerebrum.

These dogmatic dimwits are a tragic contrast to earnest, thinking people of faith. The church has a long, proud history of intellectualism: St. Augustine, Aquinas, C.S. Lewis and G.K. Chesterton to name a few. Whether you agree or disagree with their conclusions, you must take these people seriously, for they are serious, substantial people.

Not one of them would ever attend an Amy Grant concert or discuss biblical criticism with Jim and Tammy Faye.

Or starve to death in the cab of his pick-up truck waiting for God to drop him a sandwich.

According to the Associated Press, this was the "fate" of a Mr. Dewitt Allan Finlay, late of Kalispell, Montana. Finlay, a devout believer (if not an exemplary driver) got stuck in the snow on a road in the Oregon mountains on November 14 of last year. He had passed through the town of Agness just 18 miles earlier, but instead of hiking down the road or going for help, Finlay prayed for help.

And he waited.

He got caught up on some letter writing, and waited some more. He slept, he drank melted snow, he continued praying...and waiting. The snows came, the snows went. The weeks dragged on, but still he waited for a miracle.

Finally, after months of waiting, hoping and praying, Finlay was found, having heroically starved himself to death sitting in a truck that was only a few hundred yards from clear pavement and safety.

Faith teaches that there is a reason for all this, and there is: Finlay was an idiot. Yes, a devout and kind man, no doubt. His intentions were the best, I grant you. If there is a merciful God, St. Peter greeted Finlay warmly and pledged him to the most exclusive frat on Heaven's campus. But he was an idiot just the same, a Geek among Geeks, and a disgrace to the tradition of engaged faith.

Compare Finlay's ordeal to that of Capt. Scott F. O'Grady, a Christian who found himself lying face-down in a Serbian ditch while armed Slavs searched for him only a few feet away. Six days were enough for O'Grady, who put his trust in the Lord but stopped along the way to eat a few ants and suck the moisture out of a pair of socks.

After his rescue, O'Grady thanked "God and the Marines" in that order. He could also have thanked whoever taught him not to check his brain at the Church door, whoever helped him discard the Geeky notion that being dumb, devout and dead is God's plan for our lives.

One could argue (and my college roommate no doubt would) that Finlay's faith was the greater because he left the entire matter in the Lord's hands. I, however, have an image of God looking down from on high and shaking His head in amazement: "What in My name is this moron thinking...Sheesh! What do I gotta do with you people? Send Charlton Heston down with directions carved in stone: 'Thou shalt get out of thy truck and walk thy droopy derriere back to town?!' Where's Darwin when you need him?"

Of the two, it was only O'Grady--trapped behind enemy lines and thousands of miles from home--who truly needed a "miracle." But instead of waiting around for one, he dug up a few insects, sucked on a sweat sock and made his own.

June, 1995

BLOWED UP REAL GOOD

"You CANNOT write a humor column about Oklahoma City!" My wife was giving me one of her trademark glares, the one with "Where's your attorney?" written all over it.

"You just can't do it. People are too upset. You can't make fun of a tragedy like this." We have had this conversation a thousand times before; it's my theory that married people essentially have only three conversations in their entire lives: they just have them over and over again. The secret of a long, happy marriage is picking really interesting topics of conversation.

My wife and I are both writers, and one of our ongoing, never-completed conversations is about the limits of comedy: What is funny? I'm from the "nothing's sacred" school, the kind of guy who would have told Weight Watchers jokes in Auschwitz. My wife, a genteel Southern belle, believes that any joke that is actually funny is probably too offensive to repeat in public.

When I told her I was thinking about writing a column on the Oklahoma City bombing, she was horrified. "It's too terrible to write about. I still can't believe it. You just don't expect something like that to happen in OKLAHOMA!"

Yeah, I said, that's one of the things that's been bugging me. As soon as the news hit, the media was full of this "Horror in the Heartland" crap. There was Bernard Shaw doing his best James Earl Jones and saying "What makes this tragedy particularly horrible is that it happened, not in New York or Los Angeles, but in the American midwest."

I lived in Oklahoma and in New York City, and my daily expectations of getting blown up by a terrorist were the same in each

106

place: zero. This is America, not Yugoslavia. Guys in New York aren't standing around in a deli going: "Yo, Vinnie! You hear that? Sounds like another busload of schoolchildren being blown up on the Brooklyn Bridge." "I think you're right, Tony. So, you want a bagel or what...?"

More disturbing, I told my wife, is the moral element in the idea "particularly tragic," the notion that the "small town" victims of Oklahoma City are somehow more innocent, less deserving of disaster than their city-slicker counterparts. One Oklahoman interviewed on CNN said: "We never thought this could happen to us. This ain't New York; we're *good* people!"

Yeah, let 'em blow up those loud-mouthed Yankees. Do 'em some good, that's what I say.

"You know what they mean," my wife replied. "You just don't expect anything this...this, well, *important*, to happen in a place like Oklahoma City. And there were true innocents in this tragedy--the children."

Here we go again, I responded. The children were "true innocents," which implies that there were people killed by this terrorist's bomb who *weren't* innocent, who got what they deserved. I can't imagine an OKC rescue team picking through the rubble going, "Hey, Frank! That looks like Harry Smith. You remember Harry: heavy drinker, ran around on his wife, kicked his dog...Yeah, he had it comin' to him."

In a terrorist attack, every victim is, by definition, "innocent." It is the random, indiscriminate nature of these acts that makes them frightening. As soon as terrorists stop acting randomly and start making sense, they are less scary and, therefore, less effective.

Having said that, I went on, why do we think of the death of a child as somehow more tragic than the death of an adult? And I will confess that I share the feeling. I have a much stronger emotional reaction to the violent death of a child than an adult. But these feelings are wrong.

The media-driven dialogue about "special" children from a "special" place dying in a "special" tragedy makes me wonder about the perceived value of the rest of us. What are we, chopped liver?

Every day, people die needlessly--from violence, disease and stupidity. Each death is a tragedy, but we insist on measuring the value of one life against another, the tragedy of one senseless death against a hundred. The unspoken message of the media coverage of Oklahoma City was that if Timothy McVeigh had blown up a Long Island retirement village for East Coast intellectuals, the story would have been buried on the obits.

My wife grimaced. "You're not going to write that, are you?

Probably not, I replied. I can't figure out the right ending...

May, 1995

WASHINGTON HUSKIES

Sally Smith may have the toughest job in America. She is the executive director and media spokesperson for NAAFA: the National Association to Advance Fat Acceptance.

This isn't like the Dairy Board or Poultry Commission ("Fat: The *Other* Other White Meat!" or "Fat: It Keeps A Body Warm!"). No, the NAAFA promotes understanding and acceptance of the "38 million Americans who are significantly overweight."

And you thought your job sucked.

One feels for Ms. Smith at dinner parties when the inevitable questions of occupation arise:

"Er, I'm in, uh,...public relations."

"Public relations, Sally? That's great--who do you work for?"

"It's, er, uh, an advocacy group..."

"Really? Which one?"

"It's the NAAFA, you probably never heard..."

"Oh, yes! Isn't that the group for fat people...oh, uh, yes, I see....care for another cocktail weenie? Not that *you* would, particularly, I just meant...."

I ran across Ms. Smith while reading coverage of a NAAFA protest march in Washington last week. Why are fat people protesting?

It's hard to say. Perhaps they have a beef with the government, or don't feel fat people have been given a place at the table. Maybe they think they've only been tossed a few crumbs, or deserve a bigger piece of the pie. I can't imagine they were protesting President McMuffin. It was reported that NAAFA members presented a petition to the president, but I suspect it was a membership application.

Reading their placards was little help. One girthfully-challenged woman held high a "Diversity Includes Fat People" sign, another demanded "Fat Freedom Now!" But why? Are we not free to be fat? Are there corpulent criminals from the overweight underground being held as political prisoners? Free the Fat Five! Will Roseanne end up on *America's Most Wanted*?

Another group chanted, "Two-four-six-eight, see the person not the weight." Not too catchy, but far superior to "We're Fat, We're Feisty, and We're Looking for your Fridge!"

Now, I have nothing against the gravitationally-advanced. In fact, as a child I was considered "husky," which was the early 70's euphemism for "fat kid." I weighed 145 lb. in the fourth grade, and I have a wellspring of sympathy for overweight people. But I have little sympathy for whiners, with or without cellulite.

The NAAFA is yet another example of "America, the Victim." The chant "See the person, not the pounds" or whatever, is the same old plate of "excuse-ism" served with a fresh garnish. Think about what they are really asking you to do: "Don't look at the results of my lifestyle, of conscious decisions to have an extra pork chop, of afternoons flopped on the sofa watching *Oprah* and shoveling down Ho-Ho's. No, don't judge me by who I am....Look at the person I would be if I were someone else!"

The fact is, except for the tiny percentage of people who are genetically doomed to obesity, most people are fat because of what they do. Your weight is a consequence of your actions. Overeating doesn't make you a bad person, or a less valuable person or even a less pleasant person. It just makes you fat.

So why do we need an Association to Advance Fat Acceptance? I accept the fact that there are fat people. Why not an Association for the Acceptance of Stupid People, or Obnoxious People, or Habitually

Unwashed People? Is there any personal trait for which I am allowed to hold people responsible? Is it possible for anyone to be judged by their actions without having their associates threaten to rough you up? I want to reiterate that I have nothing against overweight people, until they start forming associations, at which time I feel the need to go ballistic. If I am too cynical and unsympathetic, I'm sorry. But as president of the Cynics Society, I am asking you to look beyond the jokes and see my true feelings. It's not that I'm cynical, I'm just compassion-intolerant. Can't you learn to accept my condition?

Yeah, fatso--I'm talkin' to you.

August, 1994

SCHOOL'S OUT

From the AP--"Charles Hayden wasted no time when he learned his 13-year-old son was in danger of flunking. He tutored the teen at least two hours a day, reviewing flash cards and mythology in his woodworking shop.

About eleven weeks later, more than 110 hours of study paid off when Chris passed with an 85.8 percent average. But instead of congratulating Hayden, administrators in the Hempfield Area (PA) School District charged him with illegally taking his son out of study hall 34 times for the tutoring at home.

'I'm just kind of dumbfounded,' Hayden said."

If the public school system were a horse, we would shoot it.

If it were a doctor, we would sue for malpractice.

If it were a father, we would wait until he fell asleep in a drunken stupor, bundle our children up in the night, pile them into the car and flee, stopping only long enough set his bed ablaze and forward his last known address to Lorena Bobbitt.

So how can anyone blame poor Mr. Hayden for his dumbfoundedness? He probably shares the naive but commonly-held belief that schools are in the business of teaching children. He perhaps feels some sense of "responsibility," unfathomable to government educators, for his son's education and future. He may even be one of those bourgeois right-wingers who sees some supposedly "natural" connection between an individual's efforts and his performance.

No wonder the school is prosecuting him.

Mr. Hayden is a criminal, contends Superintendent C. Richard Nichols, because he illegally denied his young son the vital educational experience of Study Hall. As a product of the government-run school system, I can testify to the value of study hall. Denying me the experience of sitting in a hot classroom with a bunch of bored teen-agers while Mrs. Snelgrove read Harlequin romances and yelped "Who's popping that gum!" would have been cruel and unusual punishment. It's called "sleep deprivation."

Mr. Hayden has discovered what every government-run school student knows from experience: The actual education of children is a school system's lowest priority. Who has time to teach kids when you're busy taking attendance at home room, making sure everyone shows up for an assembly with "Conrad Condom and the AIDs Fighters," and prosecuting parents who are trying to educate their own children?

If educating children were the highest priority of the Pennsylvania school system, they wouldn't be hassling Mr. Hayden: they would hire him. Borrow his flash cards, rent his workshop; this is what you do if you wanted kids to be smarter.

But in America, we are in unanimous agreement that our government schools don't make smarter kids, or more pleasant kids, or even more socially-conscious kids. What "public" schools do is make jobs: jobs for incompetent teachers who, if thrown into the private sector, would be instructing advanced burger-flipping at the "Want Fries With That?" Institute of Minimum Wage Studies.

It's an interesting truth that, when discussing the pathetic state of public education, even red-meat reformers give a pass to the teachers. The argument is that school administrators are evil, while lil' Miss Nellie is valiantly struggling to teach her class the three R's: Readin', Writin' and Rallyin' at the state house to lobby for teacher's pay hikes.

In fact, most teachers are incompetent. For the sake of discussion, let's take out the top 95th percentile who are rocket scientists doing their social duty; and let's lose the bottom 5th percentile who keep their jobs because they help run the NEA. What's left are a group of adults who are either:

A--not proficient enough in their chosen field to work in it (i.e., failed biologists who teach anatomy, unemployed musicians who teach band, etc) or

B--education majors who, by their own admission, have NO area of specialty, and thus are qualified to mis-instruct students in almost any subject.

But the most scathing indictment of the American "education" system is this: Mr. Hayden, a laborer who "didn't like school much" and was unfamiliar with the subjects, needed only two hours a day to teach his 7th grade son what $6,000 in taxes and several months trapped in a government-run study halls could not.

If the public school system were a parent, it would be ashamed.

June, 1995

THE LAST BUS TO HELL

Here's the question:

Parked outside is the last bus to Hell (We already have summertime bus service in South Carolina, so a "Hell" bus is redundant). There is only one seat left on the bus. Who gets it: O.J. or Susan Smith?

I've been putting this question to friends, acquaintances and grocery-store cashiers during this, the summer of the Decade's Unforgivable Crimes: the Susan Smith tragedy, the Simpson case, *WaterWorld*. While the answers varied, (after the outcome of the Citadel case, several Columbians offered the seat to Shannon Faulkner), one trend has emerged. Every white person I've asked--from New York to Newberry--has said O.J. should have a reserved seat on the bus to Hell, while every black person I've interviewed has saved a special place for Susan Smith on the Damnation Express.

Why?

The knee-jerk response from blacks has been, "We don't even know if O.J. did it." So I rephrased the question: "Assume O.J. is guilty as charged. What then?" Not one person, black or white, has changed his answer. In the black community, Susan Smith is Public Enemy #1.

While this response could be dismissed as a reaction to Smith's claim that a "black man took my babies," the people I've spoken with have been more thoughtful. "Think of the children," one older, black woman told me. "How could she do that to her babies?"

Good point. Sending your children to a six-minute, slow-motion drowning so you can "catch yourself a man" is particularly cold-blooded. These kids weren't even the cause of their mother's anger or pain, merely a lifestyle inconvenience. (As one woman reporter covering the trial told me in a fit of dark humor: "Susan Smith was a single mom sleeping with *four* different men, working full-time and with two small children....Obviously, something had to go.")

On the other hand, O.J.'s crime was of a more traditional and, one could argue, more forgivable nature--a crime of passion. His victims were adults, not "innocent children (are there ever any children in a news report who AREN'T innocent?).

I, by the way, believe the odds that O.J. is innocent are just about the same as the odds that he will be convicted: virtually zero. Believing O.J. is innocent in the face of the overwhelming physical evidence requires so thorough a disregard for facts that even some journalists are unable to do it.

What's interesting about the response from whites regarding O.J. is that the nature of the crime is never discussed. Their focus is on O.J.'s nature, on the incomprehensibility of such a "bad" action by someone living the good life: wealthy, respected and admired.

Contrast this to the story told in the Susan Smith's trial, the all-too-common tale of poverty and abuse. White people, particularly affluent white people, cannot imagine such a life and assume it to be unbearable. Thus they are more forgiving.

Black people, particularly less affluent black people, have experienced many of the tough conditions Susan faced and still cannot imagine throwing away the precious gift of a child's life. They are not ready to forgive.

This is the point of departure: If you are an elitist, if you hold "lower-class people" to a lower standard, then Smith is easier to spare. If, however, you believe that personal strength and respect for life extends across class lines, then you can judge O.J. and Susan by their respective actions. Under such a comparison, Smith is the greater villain.

As for me? I would send O.J. on that last bus to Hell for one reason only: He is a coward. He will not confess. Sure, it took Susan Smith almost two weeks to crack, but she eventually bared her soul and threw herself on our mercy. O.J. hopped in his car and headed for Mexico. O.J.'s attempt to evade the justice of man makes him my first choice for the unerring justice of the Great Beyond.

Johnny Cochran won't be there on Judgment Day.

August, 1995

REAL LOSERS

The battle royale over state-run, single-gender education came to an ugly, sweaty end when Shannon Faulkner pushed her way through a crowd of her own attorneys, handlers and hangers-on to throw in the towel. When she finally faced the cameras and called it quits, the Foremanesque Faulkner looked as if the ref had let the fight go a few rounds too long.

But who were the biggest losers?

First on the loser list are the litigating leeches in Faulkner's own corner, the $4 million dollar attorneys who pushed Faulkner into a fight that, circumstances proved, she was not prepared to win. Didn't anyone explain to Shannon's lawyers that her admission into the corp might involve vigorous exercise? Shouldn't one of her counselors have counseled Faulkner to skip a few Twinkies? On the very day Faulkner quit, rumor has it, her attorneys were pushing her to stay and suck it up.

Well, I would like to see lawyer-loudmouth Val Vojdik dragging *her* butt across campus in the 100-degree heat.

Next on the list of big losers is you. You pay taxes, right? Well, right now you're paying about $13 million dollars a year to keep Bubba's Finishing School For Rich White Boys open in Charleston. If Faulkner had succeeded, chances are slim the Converse College "School for Women Who Should Know Better Than To Try To Get In The Citadel" would ever open, thus saving taxpayers a cool $4 mil. Plus, if Shannon had stayed, there would have been more pressure on the jarheads running Camp Country Club to take it private.

Going private would mean higher tuition at The Citadel, that's true. Oh, the tears I've shed for those impoverished Citadel moms, driving their "Save the Males"-adorned Volvos to the manicurist's, forced to cancel a weekend at Bloomie's in order to pay for their son's private education.

Instead, Shannon's loss is our loss...along with the taxpayer's $17 million dollar purse.

But the biggest loser in *Faulkner v. the Flatheads* is our belief in the value of losing.

There must be some things so worth fighting for that they are worth losing for. We need people who, in losing a battle well-fought, win our respect. We need the notion of "defeat with honor."

This is particularly true here in Secessionville, USA. If any culture should have respect for defeat in defense of principle, it is ours. The ad nauseam argument about the Confederate flag hinges on this notion: The flag must fly to honor those who gave all for a cause they believed in, though that cause may have been wrong.

Yet it is the Johnny Reb crowd that whooped loudest Miss Faulkner's defeat. "What a loser!" came the cry. "She finally got what she deserved! Good riddance!" And that was just from the Attorney General's office...

If the Shannon Standard were applied to the Confederacy, why, the battle flag wouldn't just come down from the state house dome; it would be dragged through the streets and tossed into the Barnwell waste dump. After all, weren't the Confederates a bunch of "losers?" Didn't they get their gray-flannel fannies kicked from Gettysburg to the Gulf?

And, like Faulkner, didn't the Southerners fight in their own self-interest? Securing slavery and lowering tariffs are hardly charitable causes. So, what's the difference?

The difference, for the "Shave the Whale" crowd, is that Faulkner was wrong, while the Confederacy...well, anyway, Faulkner was still wrong. But should we allow our belief that she was wrong destroy our respect for her efforts to do what she thought was right?

August, 1995

Chapter 7

WHO, ME?

In The Family Way

Some choose fatherhood; others have fatherhood thrust upon them. Count me in that second group.

As I write this, my wife Jennifer is great with child--our first. Actually, "great with child" isn't quite right. Try "huge with child," or "grandiose" or "overflowing with child."

Obviously she isn't within miles of this typewriter.

Since receiving the "happy news" (I spent several hours at the gynecologist's office giving the rabbit CPR), I've realized how utterly clueless I am about the role of an expectant father. For Jennifer, there is an entire publishing empire in place to fan the fears of pregnant women. Every day, friends drop off yet another atlas-sized tome on subjects such as "How To Avoid Giving Your Baby Rare, Deadly Diseases From Your Household Pets By Constantly Reminding Your Husband to Change the Litter," and "It's Not Really Caffeine If No One Sees You Drink It."

For expectant fathers, on the other hand, the bookshelves are bare. During the entire pregnancy, I've received only one book, a gag-gift cartoon book full of stinky diaper jokes. This isn't fatherhood, it's vaudeville.

As we enter the ninth month, I'm just beginning to figure out my Daddy-to-be duties. My most important task is to assuage my wife's concerns about excessive weight gain during pregnancy. I do this by lying.

And when a pregnant woman, well into her third trimester, asks a man, "Am I fat?"--especially a man who hopes one day to sleep in the same bed with her again--what is he supposed to do? Damn straight: Lie his butt off!

A truthful response would be: "Fat? My God, woman, you're Colossal! Rotund! You're the size of a small RV! We can't get the car seat belts around you! You wear a boat cover to bed; when you leave a room, the massive air displacement causes everyone behind you to pass out. Rand-McNally is charting you for the next World Atlas! Face it: You are a BIG woman!"

Wrong answer. Try:

"Fat? No, no, no, my little dumpling. You're not fat--the BABY is fat! Why, you're skin and bones, poor thing. Have another Ding Dong...."

That's my job.

My other duty is to assure her that I still find her desirable as a woman (as opposed to merely a "womb-bearer"), though I am not allowed to express this desire physically. No matter how many times she reads it, Jennifer still doesn't buy the line that "sex during pregnancy is the best sex in the world!"

At first I thought she was afraid I might hurt the baby, (a flattering thought, really). But it turns out that my wife sees sex after conception as a waste of time. To her, it's as if she's finished the Sistine Chapel, and I want to keep painting: What's the point?

She read in a book somewhere that I'm supposed to do the dishes instead. I went through 20 gallons of Palmolive in a month.

My third and most fulfilling duty as the husband of a Mom-to-be is to listen. Until my wife became pregnant, I knew nothing about the future she believed she would have. But as she read to me from the constantly-growing pile of baby books and magazines, as she wondered aloud "do I want a boy or girl," as she worried about first steps, first words, first kisses and first loves, she told me more about her hopes for life than I had ever heard before.

Most of her dreams were delightful. Some were disconcerting, particularly comments such as "I don't think the Brady Bunch family was *that* big...." But in these late-night musings I heard from a part of my wife I would never have met if she had not become a mother.

There are, in fact, two new people about to enter my life: A new baby, who will be something like her mother, but still very different; and a new mom, who will be something like my wife, but exciting, different and new.

And the adventure continues...

January, 1993

STOP, THIEF!

At 11:10 p.m. on Saturday night, I participated in the kind of one-on-one forum that has convinced millions of Americans to toughen their position on crime.

I wuz robbed.

As I pulled into the drive of my newly purchased home, I saw someone slip from behind a parked car and crouch behind my bumper. "Oh, no!" I thought. "It's those damn student loan people again!"

When he stood, I saw in his hand a large, black revolver. Uh-oh. I slammed the door of my car and threw it in reverse, but he was already at my side. He swiftly pulled the door open and inserted the barrel of his gun. Then he requested I turn off the engine and cooperate.

It seemed like a reasonable request at the time.

My wallet was sitting on the passenger seat next to me. Even before he could ask, I began pushing it at him...so fast, in fact, that he didn't see it. "Where's your wallet, man, where's your wallet?" he demanded. He finally made out enough of my incoherent babblings to realize it was on the ground at his feet. He picked it up and ran.

"Have a nice day."

After such a traumatic experience, the average person would have been shaken, overcome with fear. Not me. I calmly strolled into the house and, in a courageous and self-controlled manner, calmly changed my underwear.

To the thief, who, I am confident, is a regular reader of mine, I must apologize for the contents of the wallet. Not a dime. There were a handful of credit cards, but each has a debt burden greater than the Russian Republic's. The only thing of value was a coupon for a free dinner at a local spaghetti joint whose food is so lousy, I'm afraid if the guy uses the coupon I could get sued for negligence.

But while he gets an "F" in substance, I must give him an "A" in form. He was a particularly competent criminal, and competence is a trait so rare I must admire it wherever I find it. My robber was excellent: he used his revolver well, held high and directly at eye level, so the lead tips of his bullets were easily seen; and he used his voice well, too, barking out clear and unequivocal commands ("Hand ova yo' wallet, white boy!"). At no point did I feel that he wanted to hurt me, and he wasn't particularly rude or abusive. He had a job to do, and he set about doing it in a workmanlike manner. Now, that's what I call a robbery.

The crooks that concern me are the idiots, the druggies, the morons. There is nothing I hold in greater contempt than an incompetent criminal. They are the scourge of society.

Think about the true inconveniences of crime, and the vast majority come from dumb crooks. Dumb crooks rob people in poor neighborhoods, taking money from people who were broke to begin with. This exacerbates the problems of poverty because the robber stays poor, while the victim gets even poorer.

During my college days when I was driving a broken-down Toyota with a coat hanger for a hood latch, some idiot busted out $100 worth of windows to steal two $5 K-Mart speakers out of my car. Hey, morons! If you're going to risk going to jail, why not rob a Lexus, or a Mercedes--you know, cars that might actually have something in them?

I used to laugh at a friend with one of those "Club" theft guards in his rusty 1978 Impala. Then he told me his car had already been stolen...twice.

Dumb crooks cause so much trouble trying to rob people, we would probably save money paying them NOT to get involved. I read an account of a robber who pulled panty hose over his head while driving to the bank. Unfortunately, he had bought some kind of colored workout hose that he couldn't see through, and he drove into a police car on the way to the crime.

One reason there are stupid crooks, unfortunately, is because of the lucrative market in stupid victims. There is currently a scam going on in South Carolina in which people get letters and phone calls soliciting thousands of dollars, and promising the recipient "a major prize" in return. "A prize," the pitch goes, "guaranteed to change your lifestyle." Several people have handed over more than $5,000 to these scammers, often giving to the same scam more than once. The lifestyle-changing prize is the knowledge that you are an idiot and should not be trusted to answer your own phone.

I, on the other hand, was an excellent victim. When I spotted the gun, I tried to flee, but when it became clear I could not escape, I immediately cooperated. No stupid tricks or panicking that might disrupt the professional at work. My demeanor said: "Hey, I'm no rube, no yokel. I'm from the Big City--I *know* how to get robbed!"

I sensed a sort of mutual admiration as he pulled the barrel of his revolver from my forehead and fled into the night. You could almost smell it.

You could definitely smell something, that's for sure.

June, 1994

121

THE NAME GAME

The gray-haired waitress, a pitcher of sweet tea in her hand, bends over our table and peers at my son.

"Ooooh, what a cute little boy! You're a little darlin', that's what you are! What's his name?"

I sigh. Then, enunciating very carefully, I say "Mencken."

She looks at me as though she smells something funny.

"Nathan?"

"No, Mencken."

"Meekin? Is that a family name?"

"No, he's named after H.L. Mencken."

Continued "problem aroma" look.

"He's a favorite writer of mine," I offer. "From the 1920's."

"Oh, *Mepkin*. What a strange name." Then, turning back to my son, "But you sure are darlin', that's what you are."

I think Mencken is a wonderful name. My son is twenty months old now, and every time I say it, I still get a thrill. This is important because everyone in my family hated the name when I picked it, and I wasn't sure if my joy would survive the onslaught of ridicule, scorn and downright nastiness I've encountered since his birth.

Back then, as a naive father-to-be, I believed that picking a child's name was an intimate and personal decision to be made after careful deliberations by thoughtful parents. Yeah, right.

The naming process actually involves hundreds of parents, friends, acquaintances, passers-by, fellow passengers on elevators--anyone you happen to meet while your wife is pregnant will claim a vested interest in the name of your future child if you allow it. Every grandma claims veto power, and every grandpa reflects on the sterling quality of his own moniker.

Total strangers even get into the act. We were in line at the grocery during my wife's pregnancy when a woman in front of us--with three snot-nosed brats all screaming "I wanna Mikky Way! I wanna Mikky Way!"--noticed Jennifer's protruding womb.

"Oh, your expecting....You're so lucky! (*That fact that a woman whose kids are, at that very moment, shoving Kit Kats down the bag boy's pants can say that <u>without</u> being struck by lightning proves there is no God.*) Is it a boy or a girl?"

"We don't know," Jennifer answers.

"Have you picked out a name?"

"We're still working on it," she says.

"Well, how about Bradley for a boy and Brenda for a girl?" the stranger asks.

"How about a bullet for your brain and a muzzle for your mouth?" I reply, or would have if Jen hadn't shoved her elbow into my diaphragm.

I know this lady meant no harm, but after awhile this assumed intimacy gets old. Besides, I believe in giving your children a name that means something, such as a family name to connect him to his history, or the name of someone you admire, some friend or famous person you hope to bring into your child's life one day.

My wife does not share this philosophy. She believes in picking names the same way you pick wallpaper. Does it flow? Does it match? Have I seen it in a popular magazine lately? These are her criteria.

When the big moment arrived and she lay in the hospital bed holding our firstborn, she let me name him Mencken. She was motivated, I suspect, by equal amounts of love and post-partum morphine from her IV drip. I seized the opportunity and had his birth certificate etched in granite before she came to.

While she and I have come to an understanding, our friends have not: "How could you name him Mencken? His schoolmates are going to beat him into tapioca every day!"

This is nonsense to anyone who has been inside a day care center in the last five years. They are fast becoming a multi-ethnic mix of unpronounceable noms de guerre. After you get past Miquel and Santarita, Mohammed and Akbar, Ho, Chi and Min, and their buddies Francois and Violetta, you think the name Mencken is a problem? Whose going to beat him up--La Quisha, Tyrolia and their brother Congoleum?

And what about the traditional "Old South" names that are making a comeback, a name system under which Ashley, Beverly and Carroll can be boys and Bobby, Jimmy and Michael can be girls? Throw in the occasional Motte, Clinch, Bomar, Letha, Alvie, Oral and Pearl, and the only kids who'll be losing the name game in the kindergarten of 2001 will be Billy and Sue.

Jennifer and I revisited this issue on September 22 when our second child was born, a little girl. After consulting several magazines, various swatches of fabric and a color analyst, my wife came up with Alexandra Gunn. Alex.

The mom is happy, I am happy, all the relatives like it and, you'll be pleased to know, it even matches the wallpaper.

October, 1994

CHECK, PLEASE!

Ask the question, "Who is more stupid--the wait staff or the people they wait on?" and the answers will likely depend on which end of the check one holds. While waiting tables in college, I became convinced Americans only went to restaurants immediately following *WrestleManiaIV* or on the drive home from their lobotomist.

TRUE STORY: I once had an older woman, a cheap, imitation mink tangled across her shoulders, order our finest "Chicken Fried Steak, young man, *medium rare!*" So I brought her a gooey, partially fried mass of cube steak, the still-sticky batter not quite "al dente."

"What is this, young man!?"

"Oh, I'm sorry ma'am. Is it too done?"

Needless to say, I was fired from that job.

TRUE STORY: I was also fired from Bush River Mall cinemas after taking the one-hundredth call asking: "What time do your Midnight movies start?" At first, I bit my lip. "Our Midnight movies start at twelve o'clock midnight, sir."

Then I graduated to: "One moment please, I'll check. [shouting across the room] Say, Ralph! What time do our *Midnight* movies start? Yeah, he want's to know about the *Midnight* movies. Yeah, the ones at *Midnight*. Any idea what time they start? [into phone] Sir, he says they start...hello? Hello?"

The final straw was a call that went something like this:

Customer: "What time do them there Midnight movies start?"

Me: "Four o'clock in the afternoon"

"OK....Hey! Wait a minute! Your Midnight movies start at four in the afternoon? That don't make no sense!"

"Well, when would you expect them to start?"

"They should start at midnight, you idiot! Why would you call them Midnight movies if they don't start at midnight?"

"I can't imagine, sir."

One phone call to the manager later, I'm unemployed.

It's been ten years since I took a drink order or "bussed" a table, but I've always had great sympathy for people in the service industry. There are a lot of stupid customers out there, people who re-order three times, send their food back twice, drink 17 metric gallons of sweet tea and then cap off the meal with: "A three dollar tip? Honey, take a dollar back--that's too much!"

Having said that...where the Hell are they finding the idiots who wait on me every day? Aren't there any Homo Sapiens left in the service sector?

TRUE STORY: My bill at a Baskin-Robbins came to $2.23. I handed the cashier a twenty and a quarter. She looked at the quarter as though I handed her a live snake. She stared at the quarter. She stared at me. She tried to make my change three times and got three different figures, none of them close. The line behind me was growing ever longer, so finally she held out two handfuls of money and shrugged.

I counted out loud: "My bill was $2.23, and I gave you a twenty and a quarter. Two cents makes the quarter. That leaves $18. Five, Ten...." When the manager finally noticed what was going on, he ran over and started yelling...at ME! When I tried to explain that his college-aged cashier couldn't subtract, she chimed in: "He's right--I told you I couldn't make change."

TRUE STORY: I was at a Bennigan's restaurant in New York City and had to put my name on a wait list. Now, Bennigan's is one of these fern-filled "Brass and Glass" cookie-cutter places that tries to serve 15 different cuisines and therefore does them all badly ("Today at Bennigan's: Blackened Sweet and Sour Fajitas!") They also do this faux-down-home crap where people waiting for their tables are called over the loudspeaker in the following manner: "Bennigan's is pleased to welcome...the SMITH party! Smith party of four, your table is ready and waiting at Bennigan's." I thought it was hokey, so as a joke, I gave my name as "Nazi," then gave my real name. Twenty minutes later, in a crowded New York restaurant with a large Jewish clientele, a paid employee made the following announcement:

"Bennigan's is pleased to welcome...the NAZI party! "The Nazi Party, come on down, your table is waiting...etc." The astonished silence of the diners was only broken by the sound of the mic-wielding employee saying: "What'd I say? I don't get it! What?"

I have nothing against stupid people in theory. The problem is, stupid people are not content to be stupid in the privacy of their own homes. The must move among us, often incognito, until one day in the middle of an important lunch meeting with your fiscal future at stake, you find yourself having this conversation:

"My guest can't eat fried food. Is the chicken on this salad fried?"

"Well, it's kind of, like, you know, grilled."

"So it's a *grilled* chicken salad?"

"Well, I mean, it kind of 'fries', like, in a pan, you know?"

"So it's fried?"

"I mean, like, it's not like Kentucky Fried. Like, it's not breaded."

"Just bring the grilled chicken plate then, please.'

"Oh, I'm sorry sir. We're all out of chicken."

"What about the chicken salad plate?"

"Oh, you can have that."

"Waiter, I thought you said you were out of chicken?"

"Only the grilled chicken."

"Oh, so the chicken on the salad is *fried...*"

"Well, it's kind of, like, you know, grilled..."

April, 1994

BOOK LEARNIN'

"The Indian...is [Nature's] inhabitant and not her guest, and wears her easily and gracefully. But the civilized man has the habits of the house. His house is a prison."--Thoreau

All my life, I've been nature's victim. In man's eternal struggle with the elements, I've been left face-down on the mat, begging for mercy. When it's homecoming weekend at Mother Nature U., I'm on the schedule.

Walking through the woods, my hands always find the poison ivy and my feet stumble across every gopher hole. Birds give me disparaging looks, chipmunks snicker and point.

Why? Because I have too much book learnin'.

That was my father's theory, anyway, offered during one of my childhood fishing trips. He said it as he watched me stab my bleeding thumb for the twelfth time while trying to bait a hook. For my Dad, fishing with me was a parental duty, not a pleasure. I talked constantly ("Scarin' them fish, son!"), and I was always getting my line hung on unseen snags, probably the wreckage of the boat I had sunk on a previous trip.

"Son, you're a bright boy, and I know you try hard. But you just don't have the feel for nature. You got too much book learnin'!"

Book learnin', for those of you unfamiliar with the South, is what pointy-headed types foist on innocent school children, useless information such as literature, art and personal hygiene. Good southern young 'uns naturally resist such indoctrination, often able to withstand 12 years of mandatory education without a single abstract idea puncturing their Confederate crania.

I, however, was an early casualty. Instead of huntin' and fishin', I took to readin' and writin'. Instead of rambling through the woods, I spent my days buried in books. The few times I was dragged along on hunting trips (I was rarely allowed to actually touch a gun), I spent most of the time losing my hat or trying to get mud out of my boots.

My cousins and uncles, who could barely count their own fingers and toes (which often totaled an odd number, by the way) but could shoot the eye out of a squirrel at 100 paces, mocked me mercilessly. These hunter-gatherers, living so close to nature, denounced me as a victim of rationalism and a Eurocentric education. They railed against the decline of sensualism in our post-Industrial society and the technological determinism that had crushed my spirit.

Actually, I'm paraphrasing. The way my Uncle Willie put it was more like:

"Boy, don't you know better than to point that goddam gun at me? And look where you're...Kee-rist, boy! Can't you even walk straight? You got all that book learnin', but you ain't got the sense God gave a piss ant."

Thoreau couldn't have said it better himself.

I began to look upon the outdoors as a dangerous, disorderly place where the intellectually unfit could prosper while the learned and urbane were marked for failure. When I finished high school, I fled South Carolina and left its rural lifestyle as far behind me as possible. My travels led inevitably to that urbane utopia, that bastion of book learnin', New York City.

I like New York. It's a city where people rule nature, a place where nature is handy but doesn't get in the way. New York has just the right amount of flora and fauna, all stored in easy-to-use containers. You want trees? Central Park. Animals? Brooklyn Zoo. Clean air? New Jer... Well, you can't have it all.

In New York, the night is bright as day. We live about the trees and drive below the rivers, rulers of all we survey. To Mother Nature, we say "Hah!"

Living in New York, I began to go through an interesting transformation. I remember walking with friends through Central Park one day and casually identifying a bird ("That's a dead one!"). My friends were so impressed, I began a nature tour on the spot, identifying trees, plants, animals--even the grain of wood in a 2x4 being used by gang members to bludgeon an elderly lady in some nearby bushes.

It was amazing: There were people in the world who knew even less about nature than I did! In South Carolina I was a home-grown city slicker who couldn't gut a fish or plow straight, but in Manhattan I was Paul Bunyan. With the barest of exaggerations, I could amaze my friends with personal anecdotes from back home, stories in which I braved the elements, lived off the land, went mano-a-mano with Big Ma Nature and lived to tell the tale.

There was "The Day I Touched A Dead Possum," the terrifying "Tale of the Rat Snake In The Road" (I hit it with both tires! Ooooh!) and the gut-wrenching "12 Cans of Vienna Sausages...And No Restrooms!"

I lived in New York for three years, basking in my new role as "Master of the Wild Kingdom," and forgetting about the humiliation of my life back in South Carolina. But not for long.

Fast forward to a summer afternoon in rural Blythewood, SC, where my new bride Jennifer and I live on two rustic acres half an hour outside Columbia. Resigned to life in the South, I have established an uneasy truce with the world of nature. Inside our fenced yard I mow, garden a bit, and sit on our deck to watch the sun set.

Outside the fence line were woods teeming with deer, birds and opossum. We left them alone, tried to be good neighbors and hoped they would do the same.

Just beyond these woods was a pasture occupied by a herd of cattle. Actually, "gang" would be more accurate for the small group of cows that prospered on this untended farm. The property was part of a disputed estate, and the care, feeding and fertilization of these cows was the responsibility of a large, dour-looking Brahma. The bull was definitely a "self-starter," and the cow population grew rapidly.

Many afternoons we would watch as the cows lumbered along our fence line, migrating to some unknown cow confab beyond the woods. They moved slowly, single file, like trucks on a city street, and always under the Brahma's watchful eye.

These were halcyon days, nature minding her business and Jennifer and I minding ours. Until...

One Saturday afternoon, we pulled into our drive and found a cow in our yard, a light-brown heifer munching nonchalantly on my wife's zinnias. As we drove forward, the cow gave us a bored glance and resumed her lunch.

We got out of the car and looked around. We couldn't figure out how she got into our completely fenced-in yard. My wife looked at me impatiently. "Do something," she demanded, taking that "This is a man problem, and you're the man" tone of voice. Men hear this tone whenever something mechanical refuses to work. Women apparently believe that men have some special genetic code that allows a CPA to turn into McGyver in the presence of an internal combustion engine.

"Well?" she demanded again.

"Hmm," I thought. "It's only a cow, right? Cows can't really hurt you--I mean they don't have retractable fangs or emit foul odors when frightened...do they? I had a moment of "Watership Down"-inspired fear that Bossy might turn on me with some undiscovered form of bovine ju jitsu.

"Calm down," I told myself. "All you have to do was get the cow back over the fence"...except I couldn't figure out how she had gotten over in the first place. I had never seen a cow jump. As far as I knew, cows had three speeds: lumbering, standing, and appearing as hip counter-culture figures in Gary Larson comic strips. Well, she had come over. She could go back.

I moved toward her timidly, all the while uttering reassuring cow comfort phrases like "Good Cow" and "That's a girl" and "Oh, gross! Did you have to do that in MY yard?" Suddenly the cow bolted! She was moving. "Yes!" I shouted.

Oh, no, I groaned.

She was rumbling directionless across our property, first toward the house, then toward the fence, then right at our new car (how do I explain that to the insurance company?). "Do something!" Jennifer screamed.

"What do you suggest?" I screamed back.

I am a reasonably competent person. I can order French food, I do my own taxes, I have even assembled children's toys. But what do you do when you have a 2,000 pound bovine Buick careening across your front yard? There's no cowboy next door ridin' herd. Who do you call? The SPCA? Burger King?

Then Jennifer had an inspiration. She pulled out our lawn mower and cranked it up. The sputtering roar from its 3 HP engine inspired a Jackie Joyner-Kersee leap, and our brown visitor was gone, disappearing into the woods. We stood motionless for a moment, mouths open. Then we burst into laughter. How could we, the modern American couple, be so helpless? This cow could have spent a week in our yard, and we couldn't move her. Thankfully, technology had the last word, and we went, giggling in triumph, into our house.

We were called back out a few hours later by mournful bellowing from under our window. "She's back," Jennifer said. "And this time she's not alone."

The cow was in the zinnias once again, only now the entire herd was gathered at the fence. With loud mooing and vigorous head-shaking, Bossy was telling them she was onto a good thing and that they ought to get smart and join her. Standing stoically amid the gang, the big Brahma himself.

We tried the lawn mower trick again, and it worked once more. But a few minutes later Bossy was back in the flower garden finishing her dessert. Worse, several other cows began vigorous stretching exercises, warming up for the big jump.

In a matter of moments, I was about to play host to the Ponderosa.

So I did the only thing I could think of: I turned my sprinkler on them.

My rotating sprinkler slowly rained on the cows like a warm summer shower. Bossy moved to her side of the fence. Other cows moved into the water for a better spot. The bull eyed me suspiciously. For an hour and a half, I watered the cows.

Finally, darkness began to fall. Without a sound, the bull gave a dull shrug and slowly moved back toward the pasture. His flock followed, confused but content.

Later that evening, as I repaired what was left of our fence, I stared nervously into the woods all around us. As far as I could see, nature had us surrounded, penned in. The animals, the cows, the woods, nature had free reign. Usually we were of little interest to them, but they could come for us any time they wanted.

Their own Bronx Zoo.

Looking back on it, for the cows it had been a day at the beach. For cow excitement, being chased by a lawn mower and sprayed down in the afternoon sun was as close to Carowinds as they would ever get. They would probably be back with soap-on-a-rope and beach towels, waiting for cocktail hour.

If nothing else, I had given them something to talk about. Years from now, at cow get-togethers, they would begin conversations with "Remember that crazy fella with the mower who turned the hose on us? He musta had too much book learnin'."

Mother Nature - 20, Me - 0.

Next time I'm firing up the grill.

August, 1993

A BIT OF HUMBUG

It's the holiday season and you regular readers out there are no doubt expecting a biting, satirical lambasting of America in the throes of its annual holiday glut-o-rama, and with good reason. It is standard operating procedure for humor columnists to crank out a "If This is the Season of Giving, Why Won't Anyone At the Mall Give Up Their Parking Space?" article the week or so before Christmas. We cynical writer-types love lampooning Christmas because the topic reveals the inherent hypocrisies of our capitalist system while at the same time allowing us to rerun a bunch of "drunk relatives" jokes.

But I am not writing a cynical, inside-the-Beltway, hipper-than-thou, wise-cracking, hyphen-riddled column.

I must confess: I like Christmas.

Yes, it's crass. Yes, it's commercial. Yes, I always get a pair of black polyester socks from my grandmother, the thin, clingy kind that stretch up to my sternum. But Christmas is still my favorite time of year.

I furthermore agree that there isn't a lot to like about the way Christmas is currently celebrated, particularly in the South, where it's not unusual to be out water-skiing and sunbathing on Christmas Eve. If the hot weather doesn't melt your Christmas spirit, try the Dixie tradition of "Drivin' Around Lookin' at the Lights," where lines of cars wait to get a peek at gaudily-festooned mobile homes decorated like a Vegas bordello run by deranged elves.

Hardly what I would call my "Christmas fantasy."

And that's too bad, because Christmas is about fantasy, about the wonderful things that could be, but never are. You could have snow! (In South Carolina? Yeah, right.) Your husband could accidentally buy you something that fits, despite your continuing claims that you're still a size four (Fat chance). Maybe this year Aunt Agnes won't bring a fruit cake the size of a Duraflame log (Dream on).

And dream we do, living again, for a day or two, in the land of the "could be," the place children live in every day.

This is another reason I like Christmas. It is the only time of year I can bear the company of small children (i.e., those under the age of 27). They are imbued with a sense of what could be. For children, every unopened present represents limitless possibilities. Every box under the tree, no matter how small, could be a bike, or a jet fighter, or a real live dinosaur. Inside every Hallmark card could be a crisp $20 bill, a letter from the president, or a ticket to Mars.

Of course, it's always underwear, or a pair of shoes, but it could be...

Watching children, plump with hope and ignorance, *is* watching Christmas, because children have the enviable ability to enjoy the things they get. They revel in the joy of having, in the pleasure of possessing. Adults, having lost this innocent pleasure, don't understand. When kids cry to take their new toys to school, we think they want to show off. No, they just want to be near their new treasures. They enjoy the having.

Grown-ups have lost the ability to relish a gift unearned. We are embarrassed when, having given someone a set of Ginsu knives or a bamboo steamer, we open their gift to us and find a beautiful watch or an expensive bauble. We cough, we gasp, we do some quick math and feel terrible. Instead of being thrilled by the generosity of our friends, we are filled with guilt. The pleasure of possessing is gone. We have only the hollow joy of giving.

This reaction, these feelings, are so apparent at Christmas. This is core of my delight in the Christmas season. It is a time when we are all so very, very human. Pretense, fear, guilt, desire, hope--most of all hope--they hang heavy upon us like the smell of a Douglas Fir in a well-warmed house. A lifetime of experience, years of punishment, realization and loss, all those truths we live by, these melt away beneath the Christmas snow.

In their place comes hope, which, for a few days, rides rough-shod over our reason, and we are children yet again.

So find me after Christmas, and we'll talk again of politics and world peace and the petty things that are.

Today, let's have the dreams of the great things that could be.

December, 1993

About The Author

Though born in Los Angeles, Michael Graham grew up in the small, rural town of Pelion, South Carolina, where he spent his formative years "running from large, hairy people named 'Bubba,' many of them women." He graduated from Oral Roberts University in 1985 with a B.A. in English Literature.

Michael worked the comedy club circuit for six years, appearing in 41 states with artists like Robin Williams, Brett Butler, Tom Arnold and Jeff Foxworthy. He has written for the *Washington Times*, *Comedy USA* and *The* (Columbia, SC) *State*. He is the featured humor columnist for the (Columbia, SC) *Free Times*, and his columns have appeared in magazines across the Southeast.

Michael is married, has two children, and is actually in a pretty good mood most of the time.